❧❧

"Help! Wolf!" he continued to shout.

From the nearest hut their father came running, fear straining his features. "Children!" he shouted, the panic in his voice clear to Ruth even through the roaring in her ears. She felt his arms reaching out for her.

"My legs are on fire, Father," she whimpered, her throat raw from crying. "Put it out."

"You're not on fire, child."

"But I can feel it. It's burning me," she sobbed. Slowly her vision faded, but she could still hear him calling her name. She tried to answer but couldn't. In the distance she could hear the howl of a wolf, and it filled her with a fear she had never known before. In her mind she pictured once again the wolf that had attacked her, from the silken gray of his fur to the piercing green of his eyes.

I never knew wolves had green eyes, she thought before darkness claimed her.

The wolf staggered away from the children, hurt and confused. It could barely breathe, and the wound felt as though it were on fire. It knew a place where it would be safe, though, a place where it could lick its wounds and wait for the dawn. Somehow it knew that things would be better with the dawn, but it didn't kn

❧

Be whisked away to another world with
these intriguing fairy tales!

THE STORYTELLER'S DAUGHTER
by Cameron Dokey

BEAUTY SLEEP
by Cameron Dokey

SNOW
by Tracy Lynn

MIDNIGHT PEARLS
by Debbie Viguié

SCARLET MOON
by Debbie Viguié

Published by Simon & Schuster

SCARLET MOON

Debbie Viguié

SIMON PULSE
New York   London   Toronto   Sydney

This book is a work of fiction. Any references to historical events, real people, or real locales are used fictitiously. Other names, characters, places, and incidents are the product of the author's imagination, and any resemblance to actual events or locales or persons, living or dead, is entirely coincidental.

First Simon Pulse edition April 2004

Copyright © 2004 by Debbie Viguié

SIMON PULSE
An imprint of Simon & Schuster
Children's Publishing Division
1230 Avenue of the Americas
New York, NY 10020

Designed by Debra Sfetsios
The text of this book was set in Adobe Jenson.

Printed in the United States of America
6 8 10 9 7

Library of Congress Control Number 2003108403
ISBN 0-689-86716-6

✦✦✦✦✦✦

To Feu Feu and Wolfie, my big, bad "wolves."

I would like to thank Lindsay Washburn for her research help.

I would also like to thank my ever-supportive husband, Scott,
and my parents, Rick and Barbara Reynolds.

Lisa Clancy, you're an editor in a million,
and I couldn't do it without you.

✦✦✦✦✦✦

✤ Chapter One ✤

The woods were changing. The cycle of death had begun yet again. What were once proud, green trees now stood half naked and clothed only in hues of fire and gold. Their gnarled branches stretched downward toward the faint path that wound below. Upon it a young girl with pale skin and black hair walked hand in hand with her older brother, unaware of the wolf that was stalking them. The trees saw, though, and whispered a warning as the wind rattled their remaining leaves.

The little girl was skipping along, her bright red cloak fluttering in the chill air. It was the color of blood and it drew the wolf in closer. Flitting like a gray ghost, it slunk along behind the trees, just steps from them, and watched. The children were close to the village; a few minutes more and they would be out of the forest. The girl turned as though she heard what the trees were whispering and shivered a little. Feeling her movement, the boy glanced back as well. The wolf circled around warily until he stood on the path before them.

When the children turned back, the wolf was

there. He lunged forward, fangs and claws sinking into the girl's legs. She screamed as it knocked her down and her own blood sprayed up into her face. She struggled to sit and came face to face with the monster.

Beside her the boy raised his dagger in the air before plunging it into the wolf's chest. The creature cried out in pain and let go of her. It jumped back, blood gushing from the wound, and stared at them for a moment before turning and staggering off into the trees.

The trees shook sympathetically, showering down leaves upon the children, covering both them and the trail left by the injured wolf. As night drew near, the trees continued to shiver, urging the children to run home, and whispering another warning.

It wasn't safe in the woods after dark.

Ruth clung to Stephen as he staggered out of the forest carrying her. With every step he took, she screamed as a fresh wave of pain washed over her. He stumbled toward the village, shouting. From their tiny homes the villagers spilled forth, drawn by his cries.

"Help! Wolf!" he continued to shout.

From the nearest hut their father, Jacob, came running, fear straining his features. "Children!" he shouted, the panic in his voice clear to Ruth even through the roaring in her ears. She felt his arms reaching out for her.

"My legs are on fire, Father," she whimpered, her throat raw from crying. "Put it out."

"You're not on fire, child."

"But I can feel it. It's burning me," she sobbed. Slowly her vision faded, but she could still hear him calling her name. She tried to answer but couldn't. In the distance she could hear the howl of a wolf, and it filled her with a fear she had never known before. In her mind she pictured once again the wolf that had attacked her, from the silken gray of his fur to the piercing green of his eyes.

I never knew wolves had green eyes, she thought before darkness claimed her.

The wolf staggered away from the children, hurt and confused. It could barely breathe, and the wound felt as though it were on fire. It knew a place where it would be safe, a place where it could lick its wounds and wait for the dawn. Somehow it knew that things would be better with the dawn, but it didn't know why.

When Ruth awoke, sun was streaming into her eyes, and her legs still felt as though they were on fire. Her first sense was one of fear, and she cried out.

"Hush, little one, you are safe," a familiar voice said soothingly. Her brother stood over her, his face twisted as if he were in pain.

"What is wrong, Stephen?" she asked.

He picked her up, hugging her to him. "Thank

God you're awake," he whispered against her cheek.

"You're tickling me," she protested.

He laughed and laid her back down. "You had us all frightened, little one."

"Am I going to die?" she asked, the fear still tugging at her heart.

"No, God be praised," her father said from the doorway.

She turned to look at him and saw tears streaming down his cheeks. The sight frightened her more than the pain she felt or the memory of the wolf that had inflicted it.

He turned his face away from her, and his voice was muffled as he continued. "You will be all right. You will even walk again, though the scars will remain."

His words frightened her still more, and she struggled to sit up. Stephen pushed against her shoulders, trying to hold her down, but she fought him. Her fingers clawed at his hands and she scratched him. At last she rose up on her elbows just as her blanket slid to the floor.

She stared in horror at what was left of her legs. They were crisscrossed with angry red wounds. Whole chunks of flesh were missing, and the marks of the wolf's teeth were clearly visible.

She dimly heard Stephen's voice telling her that everything was going to be fine. *How can it be?* she thought, her horror mounting with each passing second.

"I am hideous!"

"No! Listen to me. You are still beautiful and you will heal in time."

Ruth nodded for his sake because she could hear the pain and the fear in his voice, and it broke her heart. She would be strong for him. In her heart, though, she didn't believe him.

A movement in the corner of the room caught her eye, and she turned to glance at a cloaked figure standing in the shadows. *Grandmother?* she wondered for one wild moment. But it couldn't be, because her grandmother lived in the forest and wasn't allowed to come into the village—ever.

Outside she heard a commotion, many voices mingled together in excited shouting. She turned away from the cloaked figure as her father strode to the door and flung it open. He stood for a moment before turning with a satisfied nod. "They have the wolf."

"I want to see it," Ruth quavered, fear and hatred filling her.

"So you shall," Stephen said, swooping her up in his arms. He carried her outside. Coming up the path was a group of men who wore tired yet triumphant looks.

"We followed the trail of blood," her cousin, Peter, shouted from the head of the troupe. "We lost it, but when we searched the area, we found this wolf, already dead. He died of the wound you gave him, Stephen."

Ruth tightened her grip around Stephen's neck, her heart beginning to pound in fear as she caught sight of the monstrous gray brute. They dropped the wolf at Stephen's feet with great ceremony.

Peter reached out to touch her hand. A year younger than her brother, he was still several years older than she. His parents had died a year before, and he had been living with them since. He had grown much in that time, his body beginning to make the transition from boy to man, as evidenced by his expanding shoulders and increasing confidence.

"I cut off the wolf's paw for you to keep," Peter told her.

"I don't want it," she whispered. "You keep it."

Slowly she looked down at the body of the wolf. It was ugly, its fur splattered with streaks of dried blood and its tongue hanging out the side of its mouth. Its fangs were covered with bits of flesh. At last Ruth looked into its eyes, which were wide open and staring. They were lifeless, like two little pieces of round yellow glass.

Yellow.

A chill went through her and she buried her head against Stephen's shoulder. "It's not the same wolf."

Something was wrong; she could feel it. Two weeks had passed since the wolf had attacked, and in that time she had felt closer to her brother than ever before. He had been by her side constantly, warm and caring. The last few hours, though, he had seemed cold and aloof.

"Again," he commanded, sitting by the hearth and extending his arms toward her.

She struggled up from the edge of her bed, trying to stand. At last she gained her feet. With pain shooting through her legs, she tried to hobble using the crutch he had made for her. Since before dawn he had had her up, trying to get her to move around using only the crutch. She was getting tired and angry.

Halfway to the hearth she began to lose her footing and fell onto a chair.

"I can't do it!" she exclaimed as her crutch fell to the ground.

"You can and you must!"

"I'm tired. I'll work on it more tomorrow."

"No, you'll work on it today."

"Why? Why today?" she demanded.

"Because tomorrow will be too late," he said, standing so suddenly he knocked over his chair.

"Why?"

He sighed and dropped his eyes to the floor. After a moment he crossed over and knelt beside her. "Ruth, the duke has sent a call for men to join him as he marches with the prince to the Holy Land. They need men to fight in a crusade against the infidels holding Jerusalem."

"What has this to do with you?" she whispered,

though she feared that in her heart she already knew the truth.

"Peter and I are going. We have heard the call and it has resonated in our hearts. We will join the duke and the prince."

"But you are blacksmiths, not knights."

"And they need those more desperately even than warriors. We will help build and repair weapons and armor, and shoe horses. If need be, we will fight as well."

"You're leaving tomorrow, aren't you?" she asked, her voice trembling.

"The army leaves at first light. We are traveling to the castle tonight to join it."

Ruth threw her arms around his neck and clung to him, terror filling her. "Don't go," she begged.

"I have to," he said. "They need me."

"I need you," she countered.

"No, you are strong. You do not need me to look after you anymore. But Father will need you now more than ever. You must promise me that you will help him."

Her tears spilled out freely, running down her cheeks and soaking his shirt. "I can't."

"You can, Ruth," he said, pulling away and staring into her eyes. "You are strong and brave. Not even the wolf could beat you."

She shivered at the mention of the creature and began to cry even harder. "But you were there to protect me."

From his belt he pulled his dagger—the very one he had used upon the wolf. He placed it in her palm and wrapped her fingers around its hilt. "I will still protect you, so long as you carry this with you."

She stared from it to him, praying to find the words that would make him stay. A shadow fell across the room and she turned. Peter stood in the doorway, a sack on his back.

"I will miss you, Ruth," her cousin said, his voice trembling.

She held out her arms to him and he came to her, hugging her tightly. Then the three of them hugged, all of them crying.

Finally Peter pulled away. "It's time to go," he said softly, and Stephen nodded.

"But Father—"

"We said our good-byes this morning," Stephen assured her.

"He knew and he did not tell me!"

"We agreed it would be better this way. Nothing is to be gained by lengthy good-byes."

Stephen stood and crossed to a corner, picking up a sack that Ruth hadn't noticed sitting there. He threw it across his back before bending to kiss the top of her head.

"Be strong," he whispered. He turned to Peter, and without another word the two of them left.

Ruth sat, shaking and staring at nothing, for several moments. When she could no longer hear the sound of their footsteps, she stood slowly, using the chair for support.

She picked up her crutch and began to hobble

painfully. Every step sent pain up her legs, and she bit her lip to keep from crying out. A few steps and she made it through the door. Outside, the road was a river of mud winding between the houses and scattered shops. Smoke curled from all the chimneys, and people walked by quickly, their heads bowed and their spirits dampened by the recent rains.

The thick brown ooze clutched at her boots, and each time she pulled them free the motion was accompanied by a loud sucking sound. Slowly, step by painful step, she made her way toward her father's blacksmith shop. He was already there; she could hear his hammer ringing out against steel—strong, angry-sounding strokes.

He glanced up at her as she entered, but he said not a word. Slowly she made her way over to the forge. A steel blade sat in the fire, the metal becoming soft and pliable. With tongs she pulled it out and placed it upon an anvil.

She leaned her body against a stone pillar and propped her crutch up against the back of it. She reached down and picked up her brother's hammer. The feel of it in her hand brought tears again to her eyes. It was heavy, but she lifted it high into the air. As she slammed it down upon the glowing steel she met her father's eyes. He nodded slowly and then turned back to his own blade. Together they hammered far into the night.

⚜ Chapter Two ⚜

*T*he trees moaned and sighed as below them a deer died a sudden, violent death, its life taken by another creature. Claws and teeth slashed at the animal, rending flesh. There was nothing the trees could do but stand and watch and worry. The creature below them tore into the deer, devouring it as quickly as it could. *What a disturbance; what a tragedy; how very unnatural.*

Ruth slammed the hammer down on her thumb and choked back an oath. *Why are you so clumsy this morning?* she chided herself.

She plunged her hand into a bucket of cool water nearby. After a couple of minutes she pulled it out and crossed to a bottle that sat on a shelf across the room. She picked it up, squeezed a thick liquid onto her thumb, and slowly rubbed it in. The scent of chamomile, geraniums, lavender, lemon, myrrh, and rose filled her nostrils. The remedy was her grandmother's recipe, and it was designed to

11

alleviate swelling. Years before, Ruth had started keeping a supply of it on hand in the shop. Every finger knew it well.

She let out her breath slowly, forcing herself to relax. After a minute she stared gingerly at her hand. She grimaced at what she saw. It was rough and red like a man's and laced with scars. Through the years she had broken three of her fingers, but thanks to more of her grandmother's treatments and care, none of them were crooked.

She sighed and closed her eyes, hearing snatches of local gossip in her head. "She's never gonna find a man 'less she starts acting like a woman." The women of the village thought she didn't know, didn't hear them talking about her. She heard, though, and the words hurt.

I can fight against a sword, or fists, but I don't know how to fight against words, she thought bitterly. *Worse, I know it hurts Father, though he would never say.*

Ruth clenched her fist and watched the muscles in her forearm jump. Her grandmother had lotions for those, as well, to keep them from growing quickly. If it weren't for those creams, Ruth's arms would be twice as big.

"When Stephen returns, there will be time enough for me to worry about marriage," she muttered to herself. It was an old mantra, but it still gave her strength. She didn't let herself think about what would happen if he never did return. Eventually he would—he must. Just six months before, a young man had returned to his home in the village. He said that the fighting was still raging. Knowing her brother, he wouldn't return until it was done. Until then, she would continue to help her father and keep using salves to keep her skin smooth and soft.

Except for my hands. I wish Grandmother could do something about their redness. Ruth was instantly angry with herself for thinking it. *I have nothing to be ashamed of; I earned every one of these scars.*

Thinking of the scars on her fingers was enough to make her legs begin to ache. She grimaced as she sat down on a barrel and rubbed them. *Those scars I didn't earn,* she thought grimly. There was nothing about them to be proud of. Her thoughts flashed, as they often did, to the wolf that had caused them. *I wonder if he's still alive out there?*

Ruth shook her head to rid it of the question. The woods held enough terror for her without her allowing thoughts like that in. *No, he probably died long ago.* That thought did give her a great deal of satisfaction, and she stood, ready to continue working.

She crossed to the anvil and bent to pick up her hammer. A shadow darkened the door and she glanced up. A man stood there, his form thin beneath travel-stained clothes. His blond hair was unkempt and straggled past his shoulders.

"What can I do for you, stranger?" she asked.

"I guess I would seem a stranger to your eyes, but

I know you, Ruth," he said, his voice cracking. "Though when I last saw you, your appearance was less that of a boy and more that of a girl."

She wrapped her good hand around a metal rod used to stoke the fire. "Who are you?" she asked warily. She stood her ground as he advanced.

When he got close enough that she could see his eyes, she froze. "Peter?" she whispered.

The wraith before her nodded. "What's left of me."

"Peter!" she cried, dropping the poker and flying to him.

"Careful!" he exclaimed as she hugged him fiercely.

"Sorry," she laughed, pulling back slightly. She couldn't believe the boy she remembered had grown into the man before her. Only his eyes were the same—a soft brown, shot through with gold flecks. Even they had changed, though; a shadow was in them that had not been there before.

She glanced over his shoulder to the open door. Would her brother stride through it next? Several seconds elapsed and she could feel disappointment curling like a serpent in the pit of her stomach.

Peter just continued to stare at her, and tears slowly began to trickle down his cheeks. He looked as though he were struggling to speak. Finally he gave up and just shook his head.

"Come," she said, still gripping his arms. "I must take you to see my father. We will dine and you will tell us everything."

He nodded before clasping her in his arms once more. After a moment he pulled away with a pained laugh. "Lead on, lady."

She smiled self-consciously, brushing off her trousers hastily. She had begun wearing them long ago. They offered better protection from the sparks of the fires with which she worked and better covered the scars she carried. Seeing Peter reminded her of a time long before, when she had still dressed like a girl and behaved like one.

Quickly she dampened the fire in the forge and checked to make sure nothing else needed immediate tending. Satisfied, she took his hand and led him from the shop toward her home.

Warm memories of childhood filled her as they walked. She watched Peter as he looked around him with eyes that seemed slightly bewildered. He caught her watching and gave her the ghost of a smile.

"I never thought I would see this place again. Somehow I expected it to be different, changed."

"Like you?" she asked gently.

"Strange, the thoughts one has when far from home."

"Well, you're back now, safe. You can put such thoughts behind you."

"One day, maybe," he admitted. "But that day seems far away."

His words struck her as strange, but her worry for her brother pushed them away.

Suddenly a man cried out, "Peter!" and rushed toward them. Peter jerked and twisted toward the sound. He relaxed visibly after a moment.

"Hello, Marcus," he called good-naturedly.

Marcus embraced him and then turned. "Peter has returned from the crusades!" he shouted.

Within moments people were streaming from their homes, shouting Peter's name and rushing forward to touch him. Two men lifted him high into the air and paraded him up and down the street, laughing with joy. Ruth's father rushed up and they delivered Peter into his arms. He crushed his nephew with a happy cry, and Ruth felt tears burning her eyes.

Peter is the returning hero, but where is my brother and when may we welcome him home? She shook her head, willing herself to be patient just a while longer. *Peter will surely have news.*

Down the road her father led the impromptu parade honoring his nephew. Ruth began to walk slowly, trailing behind. In her heart a nameless fear began to form, and she felt as though a shadow had passed over her. No matter what she did, she could not shake the thought that some darkness was about to touch them all.

When she entered her home, she found her father and Peter already seated at the table. She joined them and within minutes they were all eating. She watched Peter under lowered lashes as he wolfed down his food. He attacked it, eating so much so fast that she thought surely he would explode.

Out of courtesy, her father said nothing and neither did she. Instead they both ate and watched and waited. At last Peter pushed back his plate and shifted in his chair. He lifted his eyes and they darted between Ruth and her father.

"Thank you," he said. Hesitantly he continued, "It is good to see you both, to be here again."

"You are a welcome sight to us," her father answered gruffly. Ruth glanced at him in time to see him wipe away a tear.

They sat for a moment, the silence thick with unasked questions and answers they were all afraid to hear. Finally Ruth broke it. "Tell us your story."

Peter nodded slowly. "We sailed to Spain. It was a long journey and many died along the way. From there we sailed to France, and then down the Mediterranean Sea to Acre. There we fought. Some of us went on to Jerusalem, but many did not."

"And what of Stephen?" Ruth asked at last, unable to bear it any longer.

Peter said not a word, but instead dropped his head into his hands and began to sob brokenly. Ruth stared fearfully across the table at her father, who held her eyes only for a moment before turning away.

"What of Stephen?" Ruth asked again, her voice trembling.

"He fell, outside of Jerusalem. He was killed in the battle; he died so quickly. One minute he was there and the next he was gone. They killed him and there was nothing I could do to stop it."

All she could do was stare at him as he was talking. Over and over in her mind she told herself that it couldn't be true, even as the emptiness in her heart convinced her that it was. She didn't look at her father; she couldn't just yet. Stephen was dead. They had both known it could happen. If she was honest with herself she had suspected it for years, but there had always been a part of her that held on to hope. Jerusalem was far away and the battle was doubtless long and hard.

She stared down at her hands and noticed in an almost detached way that her fingernails were cutting into her palms and drawing blood. She forced herself to relax her fingers. Tiny droplets of blood beaded on her hands and fell onto her pants. That didn't matter, though. Nothing mattered.

"Everyone loved Stephen," Peter continued. "He helped save so many. He even saved the duke's life. He was so grateful he gave Stephen some of his own armor to wear, marked with the duke's seal. I brought it back with me; he would have wanted you to have it."

He reached into his bag and pulled out a breastplate. He offered it to Ruth and she took it with trembling hands. The duke's seal, that of a crescent moon, was emblazoned on the front. She had seen its like before. She passed her hand over it and then cried out as she took a closer look. There was a red stain splashed across half of the moon.

She stared in horror, the hair along the back of her neck standing on end and a sick feeling beginning to overwhelm her. At long last she looked up, her eyes seeking out Peter's.

"It's his blood," Peter said, confirming her fear.

The fog lay heavy upon the land, covering all in a shroud of gray. Death hung thick and rank in the air, and Ruth could smell the blood of some woodland creature that had been freshly slain in the night. The earth itself was dying, the cycle of the year coming to an end as one by one the days of autumn slipped from existence, beyond the grasp of a mortal man.

As she walked the barren path the black corpses of trees appeared slowly from out of the haze. The birds that remained were hushed, awaiting the coming of the sun in the last moments of the lingering night. All was silent as the grave, and Ruth thought of her beloved brother whom she would see no more. His body lay somewhere in that distant land held by the infidels, a fallen warrior in the pope's holy wars to claim Jerusalem.

Ruth cared nothing of popes or wars or infidels; she only knew that he who had loved her best in this life had preceded her to the next, and that she would give all she owned or would ever have for one last glimpse of his precious face.

But still, she put one foot before the other, moving on just as nature and all of life did and must. Far off in the woods a branch snapped. Almost unconsciously her hand tightened around the hilt of her brother's dagger. It was hers now; he would never return to claim the dagger, the very one he had used to save her from the wolf so many years before.

She peered into the darkness, wishing for the eyes of an animal so that she might see what they did. Nothing moved, at least not that she saw. A shiver danced up her spine and she turned her eyes back to the path. As she continued to walk her legs tingled slightly where there were scars. They too had never forgotten the feel of the wolf's fangs.

In a sack upon her back she carried her brother's armor. She couldn't think about it, though, or she would start crying again. Lost in thought, she didn't see the body until she was nearly upon it.

She jumped and let out a startled yelp as she realized that a man lay across the path. He lay still, as though he were dead, and he was completely naked.

At her cry he stirred and then suddenly jumped to his feet.

"Who are you?" Ruth gasped, averting her eyes.

For one moment he stood, panting like a wild deer, before turning to flee into the woods.

"Who are you?" she shouted after him.

Only silence met her question. She strained her ears but could hear nothing. *Is he hiding just out of sight, watching me?* she wondered. The thought sent a chill of fear through her. She clutched her dagger tighter and hurried on.

Who could he have been, and why was he asleep naked in the forest? Questions crowded her brain, each demanding to be heard and answered. Above her the trees began to whisper to themselves, and she could feel the hair on the back of her neck rising. She realized that her heart was pounding in fear, and she broke into a stilted run. At every step the armor banged against her back, a painful reminder of her grim errand.

Above her the trees continued to whisper and sway; dark warnings crowded her mind, and she did not know if they were real or imagined. Faster her feet flew, the path familiar to them as it twisted through the trees. At last she slowed as she neared her destination.

Ruth's grandmother, Giselle, lived deep in the forest. Her house stood, proud and alone, in a small clearing. As Ruth came into sight of it she saw smoke curling slowly from the chimney, blending with the fog until the two were indistinguishable.

The door hung a little crooked so that all manner of insects found their way underneath and inside. Grandmother always just sighed and carried them outside. There was not a straight board in the whole of the house. Giselle was gifted at many things, but carpentry was not among them. Still, she took pride in having done all the work herself.

Not that she had a choice, Ruth thought bitterly. Her grandmother had been banished from the village before Ruth was born, amidst accusations of witchcraft. It was a miracle the villagers had been content to only banish her and not burn her. Ruth shook her head. *Grandmother is no witch; she just asks questions no one else will and manages to find the answers.*

Ruth reached the door and knocked lightly before pushing it open. "Grandmother?"

"Hello, dear," the old woman called cheerfully. She was stirring something in a large pot hanging over a crackling fire.

Ruth carefully set down her sack and walked over. "What are you experimenting with now, Grandmother? Another healing potion, or a fertilizer for your garden, perhaps?"

"Breakfast," Giselle said with a chuckle, her blue eyes crackling with good humor, "and you're just in time to join me."

Ruth wrinkled her nose. "I already ate," she fibbed.

Giselle clicked her tongue. "What have I told you about lying to me? You'll have some—it won't kill you."

"That's what worries me," Ruth said with a sigh. She sat down on a chair and looked around the house. It was cluttered, as always, with all of her grandmother's things. Row after row of glass jars lined crude shelves. They held a variety of plant life that Giselle used in making her salves and ointments. On a small table were still more jars of different-colored oils. Several pots hung around the hearth, and there were more contraptions and jars spread around the room haphazardly.

On one wall hung a large piece of parchment with black dots marked upon it. Ruth knew they represented the stars in the summer sky. Mapping the stars was one of her grandmother's latest projects, and on several nights she had managed to enlist Ruth's aid.

"I didn't expect you until Thursday," Giselle commented as she removed the boiling pot from the fire.

Ruth nodded, her throat tightening as her eyes drifted to her sack.

"What is it?" Giselle asked sharply, as though sensing Ruth's change of mood.

"Peter came home yesterday from the crusade."

Giselle lunged forward with a cry of excitement. She hugged Ruth tightly and when she pulled back tears of joy were filling her eyes. "And Stephen?" she asked after a minute.

"They killed him," Ruth sobbed.

The tears of joy turned to tears of sorrow as they held each other and cried.

After eating, Giselle reverently removed Stephen's armor from the sack Ruth had brought. As Ruth again caught sight of the bloodstained moon, she shivered.

"It was given to him by his lord, as a reward for his service," Ruth explained.

Giselle nodded slowly. "I can see that." She passed her fingers lightly over the moon. "I saw a scarlet moon once, when I was a child. It rose in the night sky, the color of blood. My mother told me it was a bad omen, a marker of death. I didn't believe her then, though I confess this makes me wonder now if maybe she was right." She shook her head.

"Can you do something with it, make it into something I could wear?" Ruth asked, her voice hoarse from crying.

Giselle nodded. "I'll see what I can do."

"Thank you."

"Maybe I can make something you can wear for protection as you walk through the forest."

"You're the one always telling me I have nothing to fear from the woods."

"It's not the woods I'm worried about," Giselle said meaningfully.

Ruth had almost forgotten about the man she had seen earlier, but her grandmother's words reminded her. "I saw a man on my way here today. He was lying naked in the path. He woke up and ran away before I could get a look at his face."

"Are you all right?" Giselle asked, voice filled with alarm.

"Yes, only puzzled."

"Some mysteries we should not seek the answers to," Giselle said ominously.

"What does that mean?"

Giselle smiled, but Ruth could tell it was forced. "Nothing. I'm just glad you're all right. And don't go chasing young men into the woods. There's only trouble to be found there."

"Grandmother, are you warning me about men?" Ruth asked, embarrassed and vaguely amused at the same time.

"I should be; most of them are ill-intentioned toward young women. That's not what I meant, though. I meant don't go chasing after strangers. They can be dangerous, especially ones running around in the forest like animals."

"I won't," Ruth said, trying to keep her voice light.

There was a knock at the door and Giselle rose to answer it. She held it wide as a young man and woman entered with their heads bowed reverently.

"Mary, James," Ruth said, nodding to them both.

They murmured greetings in return. Mary and James were the only ones besides Ruth who visited Giselle. They came to learn from her, and she had taught them much about medicine and nature. Ruth was the only one who knew they were study-ing with her grandmother. The villagers might not begrudge a girl calling on her grandmother, but they would be quick to condemn two people calling on an accused witch.

"I should go," Ruth said softly.

"No, stay and we shall explore the mysteries of nature together," Giselle urged.

Ruth hesitated for a moment. It was Sunday, so there was no work to be done. Normally she would have spent the day with her father, but he and Peter were doubtless catching up. There was nothing she could do at home, and the truth was, she didn't want to go back quite yet.

"Thank you," she said.

Giselle smiled.

For the rest of the afternoon they studied some of the deadlier plants, Giselle warning them how to spot the poisonous ones and how to make some of them safe. Ruth should have been fascinated, but her mind was elsewhere, on a lonely field outside of Jerusalem.

The tears coursed down her cheeks, and she let them. This was the only place such tears were welcome. In the village she had to be strong, both in the shop and at home. Her father did not welcome tears, believing them to be a sign of weakness. Weakness was a privilege that Ruth had given up the day Stephen left for the crusades. Her father was a kind man, but he kept his emotions hidden.

When she was younger he had been a little warmer, but the departure of her brother had been hard on him. Though he only reluctantly accepted her help at the shop, he did treat her as more of a man than he wished she was.

He wishes I would act more like a young woman. Yet, where the work is concerned he treats me like a man. I guess it is the only way he can reconcile the thought of a woman working at a man's job. Things might have been so different. How would my life have played out if I had never gone to work at the shop, if I had never learned to fight, if Stephen had never left?

Stephen. Over and over in her mind she imagined her brother dying, run through with a sword on a bloody field, his body falling slowly to the ground. In her mind she saw his eyes as he died, the love and hope fading slowly from them until there was nothing left.

"Monkshood needs to be avoided at all costs," Giselle said.

Ruth snapped back to attention and watched as her grandmother displayed a plant with deep green leaves and clusters of dark blue flowers.

"This one brings only death, swift and ugly. The tiniest amount of it can cause numbness, and a little more can cause death. It is popularly used as a poison. It grows in moist soil. I haven't been able to find a single positive use for it yet."

James turned noticeably paler. "What do you experiment on?" he asked, his voice quavering a little.

Ruth bit her lip to keep from howling with

laughter. She knew all too well what the answer was going to be.

"I will tell you when you are ready to know," Giselle answered.

James's eyes widened in alarm and Mary gave a little gasp. Ruth hid her smile behind her hand.

At least Grandmother can still make me laugh, she thought. The truth was, Ruth herself didn't know what Giselle experimented on. For a while she had suspected it was animals, but her grandmother cared too much for the woodland creatures to risk harming them.

Then Ruth had thought her grandmother experimented on herself, but that seemed too dangerous and ill-conceived to be true. At last she had come to terms with the fact that she likely would never know. *I would tease her and say she experiments on the townspeople, but given their hatred of her, and her banishment, she would likely find it painful rather than humorous.*

"Well, I believe that will be all for today," Giselle said at last. Her voice sounded strong and clear, almost cheerful, but Ruth could see the pain and exhaustion in her eyes. In one day she had found one grandson and lost another.

Ruth rose and went to her grandmother, throwing her arms around her. The action startled Mary and James, who were unused to seeing such open displays of affection.

"I'll be all right," Giselle whispered against her ear.

Ruth nodded, sniffing slightly as she pulled away. Giselle reached out a hand and caught one of her tears. "Do you need to stay here tonight?" she asked, eyes loving and concerned.

"No, I should go home. Father needs me more than ever."

"Then go, and be safe."

Mary and James rose from their seats on the floor and said their good-byes. Together, the three of them left the cabin. Outside the cabin they parted ways. As Ruth faced the path she would take back through the woods, she shivered.

It was near dusk when the three left the cabin in the woods. Two went their own way, by a path known only to them, and they were safe. The third walked the same path she always walked, and the trees were afraid for her. It was not safe in the woods—a predator lurked just out of her sight.

The trees whispered, the trees moaned, but still she ignored them. At last a wind whipped up, and as it passed through their limbs the trees began to shriek. She looked up, her face white with fear.

Yes, hurry home, child. Your father is waiting and the wolf is close behind. She broke into a trot and they whistled, encouraging her. *Faster, he is close at hand.* One of them sacrificed a branch, letting it fall scant feet from her. She screamed and began to run.

Satisfied, the trees began to whisper again amongst themselves.

Ruth was drenched in sweat when she burst out of the forest. She panted as she slowed slightly, her eyes fixed on the village. Heart pounding, she forced her tired legs to keep moving.

Why am I so afraid? she wondered. *'Twas only a falling branch.* No matter what she told herself, though, she couldn't shake the feeling that it had been something more than that. *There are times when I hear something—a whisper, a voice—like the trees are trying to tell me something.* She shuddered as she slowed at last to a walk. *The first time I heard it was the day the wolf attacked.*

She stopped just short of her home, not yet ready to go in and see her father and Peter. She stood, still winded, trying to banish the fear from her mind, but it was hopeless.

It doesn't matter what else I'm feeling, the fear is always there. If I'm happy, there is still the fear. If I'm angry, there is still the fear. She closed her eyes and forced herself to breathe more slowly. *And if I'm sad, the fear is overpowering. No matter how strong I am, how much I can lift, or how well I can fight, I'm still afraid.*

She turned and glanced over her shoulder with a shudder. The trees looked like ghosts as the evening fog rolled in. They swayed and shook, though she felt no breeze. Haunted—that's what the woods were, at least for her. For a moment she thought she saw something slipping between the trees, a gray phantom. *It's just one more of my ghosts,* she thought. *To me, there will always be a wolf in these woods.* She turned away and forced herself to take the last few steps home.

⁂ Chapter Three⁂

Ruth mopped the sweat from her brow and marveled at how much hotter the forge seemed than usual. The air in the shop felt superheated and she was having a hard time catching her breath. *Today a skirt would have been helpful, at least cooler than trousers,* she thought.

"I'm heading over to the parson's place," her father grumbled.

She glanced up with a smile.

"I thought having my own shop, a place where I could work and people could come to me, meant that I wouldn't have to go out so often."

"What needs to be done?" she asked.

"One of the large candlesticks is bent and wax is dripping onto the altar, apparently."

"I could go if you like," Ruth offered.

"No," he said, not even stopping to think about it. "You stay here. Simon should be by to pick up those blades a little later. Make sure he pays."

"I will," she promised.

Ruth watched him leave with a trace of envy. Her father hated leaving the shop to perform his job elsewhere, but she could use a change. He would never let her go, though. He was already concerned enough about her image. Having her out working in the public eye would just make it worse.

She turned back to what she was doing. Now that Peter was home, he might begin to help out as soon as he felt stronger.

After working for nearly an hour, she heard foot-steps behind her and turned to see a tall, burly man enter the shop.

"Good afternoon, Simon," she said.

Simon, a tanner by trade, grunted in reply. "Your father here?" he demanded.

"No, but your new blades are ready," she said, nodding toward one of the worktables.

He crossed and picked one up, examining its edge by running it lightly along his thumb. Even from a couple of feet away she could see the thin line of blood that appeared with the blade's passing. It gave her a good feeling to see the sharpness of her blades and to know that her work had paid off.

"They'll skin a deer twice as fast as your old ones," she asserted, moving toward him.

He tucked the two blades into the back of his belt before sucking the blood from his skin. "I'll take them because I need them, but I won't pay for such shoddy work."

"Shoddy work!" she exclaimed, cut to the quick. "I assure you both my father and I worked on them, and they are the finest blades in these parts."

"I figure a woman would think so," he grunted, giving her a withering glance. "Tell your father that when he can make better blades I'll pay for them," he said, starting toward the door.

"You'll pay for these now," Ruth told him, moving between him and the door.

"Out of my way, girl, before you get hurt."

She balled her hands into fists at her side and braced herself. She might be afraid of wolves and woods, but common men didn't frighten her. "I know you, Simon, and I won't be the one getting hurt."

"Run home to your father, girl. Maybe if you ask nice he can find a husband for you, if there is a man out there willing to bed you."

"You swine!" she shrieked. She lunged forward and hit him, hearing a crunch as her fist connected with his nose.

He staggered back with an oath, his hands flying to his face. Then with a roar he lunged toward her. She sidestepped and boxed his ear as he lumbered past. He turned, one of the skinning knives in his hand, and was about to come at her again when a man strode into the building and stepped between them.

"Good sir, you will pay this lady what she is due and leave this place." The stranger was tall and very well dressed.

"And who might you be?" Simon asked with a bloodstained sneer.

"William, Earl of Lauton."

Simon turned pale and took three quick steps backward. "I'm sorry, milord," he muttered, dropping his eyes.

Simon dug into a pouch at his belt and placed three coins on a table before turning and stumbling out of the shop. Ruth snatched up the coins and contemplated throwing them at his retreating back, but she took a deep breath and clutched them tightly in her fist instead.

"Did he hurt you?" the earl asked after a moment.

"No," she spat. "And if you hadn't interfered I might have knocked some sense into him. Now I'm just going to have to deal with him later."

He laughed out loud, his eyes dancing. "My apologies, milady. Next time I will just stand back and watch."

"Thank you," she said, taking a deep breath. They stood still for a few moments as Ruth tried to force her body to relax and her heart to slow. She found it hard to do under his watchful eye.

At last she turned and looked at him closely. He was tall; her chin only came up to his chest. His wavy brown hair just brushed his shoulders. His skin was bronzed, with the look of one who spent much time outdoors. Then she looked into his eyes and her heart skipped a beat. He had the most mesmerizing green eyes she had ever seen. There was something magnetic and exotic about them, and she felt as though she were drowning in their depths.

She forced herself to break the contact as she realized that her heart was still racing but for an entirely different reason. Perhaps it was that realization that startled her into remembering her manners. She began to curtsy, but then remembered she was not wearing a skirt. She blushed for one awkward moment before finally bowing deeply. When she stood back up, Ruth thought she caught him smiling. "I'm sorry, milord, you caught me at an inopportune moment. I did not mean to offend you."

"Don't do that," he said softly.

"What?" she asked, startled.

"Don't remember that you are a blacksmith and I am an earl. I liked you better when you didn't care a whit who I was."

She found herself smiling despite herself. "You'll have to forgive me; I often have a different view of life than others."

"Of course you do; you're a woman in a man's clothes and with a man's work. You're a lady and a blacksmith. I praise your father for his courage in raising you as both."

She shook her head, bemused. "I'd give you these coins to hear you tell him that."

"I shall tell him, and you can keep the coins."

"What is it you came for, William?" she asked, daring to use his name and knowing how many would be shocked to hear her do so.

He smiled his approval. "My horse threw a shoe not twenty paces from your door."

"Well then, that is fortunate for both of us," she answered.

"Yes, it would seem so."

"Fetch your horse and put him in that stall," she said, pointing.

He bowed low before disappearing outside. She didn't have even a moment to collect herself before he reappeared, leading a magnificent black stallion.

"Beautiful," she murmured almost involuntarily.

"Are you referring to me or the horse?" William asked with a wink.

She laughed and fought down the urge to throw something at him. "My, aren't we arrogant. I was, of course, referring to the animal."

"Then, you were talking about me," he said, his smile gone in an instant and his eyes glinting with a hard light.

Her breath caught in her throat as she stared at him. In that moment it was easy to see him as an animal—a wild, dangerous creature that would consume her if she only let him.

Then the steely look was gone and the smile again in its place. He led the horse into the stall and secured it. Ruth brushed past him and entered the stall.

"Which shoe?"

"Left foreleg."

"Easy, boy," she crooned as she slid her hand down the horse's silken leg.

When she reached his hoof he lifted it for her without a fuss. "You have lovely manners," she told him.

"He learned them from me," William offered.

"You sure it wasn't the other way around?"

He guffawed, sounding for a moment like a horse, and she laughed quietly to herself. She studied the horse's hoof for a moment.

"You treat all your customers this way?" William asked.

"No, you're special."

"And here I asked for no special treatment," he teased.

"Well, that will teach you."

"Anything I can do to help?"

She let go of the hoof and straightened. "Hand me one of those files on that table. His hoof needs to be shaved a little before I can put on a new shoe."

William hurried to do as she asked. She slid her hand down the horse's leg again, and this time he picked his hoof up before she asked. Holding it steady between her knees, she filed the edge down. As she leaned slightly into the great beast's shoulder, he nickered softly.

"He likes you," William said, his tone sincere.

"The feeling is quite mutual. He's a wonderful animal."

She returned the file to William. "Can you get me one of the shoes hanging from the first nail on the wall, closest to me. I also need a hammer and some nails from the table below it."

He grabbed the things she needed and handed her the hammer, the shoe, and one of the nails. He stood close at hand with the rest.

She fitted the shoe onto the stallion and drove the first nail into the hoof easily. William placed the next one into her outstretched hand, brushing her fingers with his own. Her skin warmed at the contact, but she tried not to think about it.

Ruth finished quickly and patted the horse on the shoulder. "Thank you for your assistance," she told William as she let herself out of the stall.

"The pleasure was mine," William said with a smile. "What do I owe you?"

She shrugged. "Let's call it even. After all, you did save me from having to kill the tanner."

The smile disappeared, and the steel returned to his gaze. "Dear lady, I would have killed him myself before I would have let you stain your hands with his miserable blood."

She didn't know what to say, so she just stood, staring mutely into his eyes. Suddenly he bent closer, and for one heart-stopping moment she thought he was going to kiss her. Instead he whispered low and fierce, "Thank you."

"For what?" she breathed.

He smiled grimly and shook his head before moving to the stall and leading his horse out. He left the shop without a word or a backward glance. Ruth walked to the door and watched as he mounted his horse and rode off. Puzzled and feeling slightly dazed, she turned back inside and saw a small pouch sitting on the table next to the file she had used on his horse's hoof.

She picked it up and gasped when she saw that it was filled with coins. "Thank you," she whispered.

William's head was spinning as he galloped his horse toward the castle. The girl had seemed so familiar to him; something about her had called to him, but he didn't know what it was. He hadn't even found out her name, though her face would forever haunt his dreams. For a moment he had been able to forget all the darkness in his life and he had felt truly free.

Freedom was not his, though, no matter how much he yearned for it. *Mine is a life already destined, the course of my future plotted, thanks to the actions of my ancestors and this legacy they left me.* He cursed his fate as he spurred his mount on.

Minutes later the hooves of his steed clattered on the stones in the castle courtyard. He slid from the stallion's back and tossed the reins to a waiting servant.

He strode into the main hall of the castle, his boots causing hollow echoes to sound throughout, until he reached the great wall, where a portrait of each marquis of Lauton hung. His father's was at the end, and next to it was a space where William's would one day hang when his father was dead and he, himself, was marquis.

He glared at the wall. Four centuries of Lautons all stared back at him, their eyes accusing him as they always did. "I have done nothing to deserve this," he hissed.

He looked at each portrait in turn, beginning with the first—William, his namesake. All of them had the same strong jaw, the same high cheekbones, the same wavy hair. There was one thing that not all of them shared, however. The first six Lautons did not have it, but all the rest did. All the rest had a darkness to them, a hungry, predatory look in their eyes. William knew that look; he had seen it in his own eyes when staring into pools of water.

The eyes mocked him, and he hated them for that. He turned back to the first portrait with those eyes and stood before it for a long time, unmoving. Finally, in a voice hoarse with rage, he asked, "Why?"

The portrait, as always, refused to answer.

As Ruth sat down to dinner with her father and Peter she placed the coins from her day's work upon the table. Her father took one look at the large amount and raised an eyebrow.

"Something happen today at the shop?" he asked.

"Yes," she answered, helping herself to a chicken leg. "Simon the tanner didn't want to pay for his skinning knives. He claimed the work was shoddy."

Her father turned three shades of red before he

finally spit out, "That was some of the best work we've ever done!"

"I know," she answered around a mouthful of chicken.

"What did you do?"

"I hit him a couple of times before he got his guard up."

"Ruth, what have I told you about fighting?"

"I know, Father, but I was safe. He didn't touch me. It turned out he didn't even have a chance to try. Lord William came by and ended the fight. Simon paid and left as fast as he could."

Her father's face went from red to white faster than she would have dreamed possible. "The marquis's son caught you fighting?"

"Yes, father," she said, dropping her eyes to her plate.

"Did he say anything?"

Ruth was in trouble and she knew it. Her father had always warned her about how to behave in front of nobility, when and if she ever met any. He had also told her repeatedly that if any strangers dropped by the forge while she was alone she was to tell them she was only there bringing something to her father, and that she should leave immediately and run home to get him. She took a drink of water, debating what next to say.

"He had heard Simon and me arguing, so it was no use pretending I didn't work there. He had come by to have one of the shoes replaced on his stallion. I did the job and told him there would be no charge since he had helped me with Simon. He left this bag of coins anyway."

She sat silent, watching her father as he stared off into space. "Lord William has a bad reputation, but it's for being a fighter and a dangerous man. If he were going to make any trouble for us regarding a woman working in the shop as a blacksmith, it would have come already."

"I met men in Acre who knew him. They had no kind words," Peter said quietly. "He's dangerous. You should try to stay away from him, Ruth. You may not be so lucky next time."

"Yes, if you see him again, be polite but try to stay away from him, and tell me as quickly as you can," her father instructed.

Ruth nodded but didn't say a word. They ate the rest of the meal in silence, and Ruth was relieved when it was time to retire for the night.

She lay down, but sleep was a long time coming. When the darkness finally did claim her, she dreamt of William and the way his eyes shone when he laughed.

William couldn't sleep. He prowled the castle, thinking. He stopped again in front of the great wall and stared at the portrait of his father. At last he turned from it, weary.

His father was off again, fighting in Jerusalem. He had come and gone often throughout the last nine years, and he had always left William home to watch the castle and guard the lands and titles. It had been a great burden his father had placed upon him, but it was nothing compared to the burden that they all shared. It was the dark secret carried by the men of the family that drove his father to return again and again to Jerusalem. *Does he seek revenge or redemption?* William wondered.

He didn't know; he and his father barely spoke even when they were both in the same room. *We keep to ourselves, even when among our own kind.*

He turned and continued pacing, his stride long and loose, his hands swinging easily at his sides. His eyes probed the darkness, seeing everything, even though he didn't need to see in the dark to move around this castle. He knew the layout so well he could walk it with his eyes closed.

At last he moved outside, the walls of the castle no longer able to cage him. Under the stars he breathed in deeply, sucking the night air into his lungs. He threw back his head and stared up at the sky. The moon was a crescent in the darkness and he stared at it, hating it and yet unable to ignore its beauty.

He paced slowly toward the stables, approaching them from downwind. The horses began to move restlessly, and he could smell their fear. Unable to smell him and know that it was William who approached, they were anxious, sensing only that a predator was near.

By the time he walked inside, they were whinnying

in fear and kicking the walls. He stood for a moment, watching them, before he called out gently. The horses instantly quieted upon hearing their master's voice. He walked down the center aisle, meeting each of their eyes in turn.

He exited the stables and continued on to a pasture beyond. The stallion the girl had shod trotted up to the fence and thrust his nose into William's hand.

"You don't belong inside, penned up like the others, do you?" William asked quietly, rubbing the velvety nose. "Neither do I. That's why we get along so well, you and I."

William sighed and leaned against the fence. "So, what did you think of her?"

The horse bobbed his head up and down, making William smile. "I liked her too. I've never met a woman quite like her. You know, I believe she could have killed that tanner." His smile faded as a shadow crossed his mind. "I am happy that she did not have to, though. No one should have to live with that kind of pain."

The stallion lipped at William's collar, and he twisted his hand in the horse's mane. "So, Shadow, what am I going to do about her?"

Shadow had nothing to say about the matter, and William sighed. "If I am anything of a gentleman, I will leave her alone."

The stallion made a chuffing noise that sounded like laughter. "Thanks," William said sarcastically. "At least I always know where you stand." He pushed away from the fence, giving the horse one final pat. "Both of us should get some sleep if we can."

He walked slowly back inside the castle, his heart weary. The girl was better off without his interfering in her life. He was the kind of trouble she didn't need. Knowing that didn't make him feel any better, though, and didn't make it any easier for him to ignore the feeling that she was someone he could really care for.

✤ Chapter Four ✤

A cold wind whipped through the shop and blew a shower of sparks about. Ruth could taste winter in the air, hard and clean. It was coming, though not yet arrived. The sun shone for fewer hours a day, and its heat did not warm as thoroughly as it had a few weeks before.

Much had changed in Ruth's life even as one season gave way to another. Sometimes it felt like her whole world was coming to an end. She turned her head slightly and stared at Peter from under lowered lashes. He had asked to come to the shop to help her out, but so far he had mostly sat, staring off into space. *Where does he go when he's like that?* she wondered. She wanted so badly to question him about everything he had seen and done in the years he had been gone. Every time she tried to ask he just shrugged and smiled weakly at her. *Why won't he talk about it? He hasn't even told me about the battle where Stephen was killed.*

Peter's body had begun to heal with rest and food, but his spirit still seemed wounded. Worse, there was no remedy she knew for that ailment.

She put down her hammer for a moment and plunged the strip of hot steel that would be a sword into cold water. It hissed and steamed as it cooled.

"I would like to go see Grandmother," Peter said, speaking suddenly.

Ruth jumped, surprised by the sound of his voice. "Then go. I know she is eager to see you. You've been home three weeks and I know she is growing anxious."

"I know; I just wasn't ready before. Would you go with me?" he asked.

"Of course," she replied, wondering why. *Perhaps he is not sure he remembers the way, or perhaps he does not wish to walk through the woods alone.*

"We can go this evening if you like."

"That would be good."

He fell back into silence, and she returned to her work, trying to shrug off her concern for him.

It was nearly time for the midday meal before he spoke again. "How is she?"

"Who?" Ruth asked, again startled and momentarily confused.

"Grandmother."

"She's well. I think you'll be surprised. She doesn't look any older than when you left."

Peter nodded. "I guess that's witchcraft for you."

Ruth bristled. "She's not a *witch*! Peter, how can you believe such a thing?"

"Isn't it true?" he asked, looking genuinely perplexed.

"It is not. She has never had anything to do with

witchcraft. It is only superstition and fear that made people misunderstand her."

"My folks included," Peter said. "They didn't let me see her much."

"I'm sorry, Peter," Ruth said, softening. She had forgotten how narrow-minded his parents had been.

Peter stood up and walked over closer. He leaned up against a table beside her. "So, what is she?"

"She's . . . just a person who is . . . interested in . . . studying," Ruth said, finding herself at a loss for the words to explain.

"Studying what?"

"Everything—plants, animals, the stars in the sky. She's even done some wonderful work with medicine and studying the human body."

"Really?" Peter asked, his voice reflecting heightened curiosity.

"Oh yes, she makes wonderful salves for burns, cuts, all manner of things."

"So, she can make people better?"

"Absolutely."

"Then she also knows what makes them sick."

"Yes," Ruth answered, not entirely sure where Peter was going with his questioning.

"I would like to learn that," he said quietly, almost to himself.

"She would love to teach you," Ruth said, laying a hand on his arm. "She has taught me so much and yet there is so much left to learn."

"Really?" he asked, his eyes probing hers.

"Yes."

"Does she teach anyone else?"

Ruth hesitated for only a moment, her thoughts on Mary and James, before she answered. "No."

He smiled wanly. "Since I have come back I have found that I am in need of something on which to focus my thoughts, my energies."

Ruth smiled. "We will go tonight and you can speak with her about all of it. Now, I have to finish this by the end of the day or Father will be speaking to *me* about something."

Peter laughed, though the sound was empty and hollow to her ears. They shared some cheese and bread Ruth had brought from home, and then she returned to work.

Peter fell back into silence for the rest of the day. Ruth glanced at him from time to time, wishing she could reach him. At last the day was over. They went home to say hello to Ruth's father and to eat a quick meal.

Then they set out into the woods, heading for their grandmother's house. Ruth carried a lantern with them to ward off the gathering shadows. It would be fully dark when they returned, and they would be sorely in want of some light.

She shivered. The woods at night was not something to be taken lightly, and her thoughts raced ahead of her, mapping out every footstep of their way. She walked several steps ahead of Peter, inexplicably not wanting to be too close to him.

You're being silly, she chided herself. *He's your cousin. There is nothing to fear from him.*

From overhead she heard the flapping of wings. She glanced up and saw a huge owl silhouetted briefly against the sky. It then landed on a nearby branch and stared at them with great, unblinking eyes.

"Who, who?" the owl called.

She was reminded yet again of the young man she had seen in the woods and how she had called the same question out after him with as little answer as she was giving to the owl.

"Ruth," she whispered. At least she could answer the owl. Maybe one day he would help answer *her* question.

They walked quickly and soon arrived. The door was open when they reached the cabin, and Giselle was standing outside with open arms. Peter went to her after a moment of hesitation and was folded into her embrace. Ruth stood and smiled weakly, fighting back tears. *I wish Stephen were here for this reunion.*

At last they all bustled inside. Candles were lit all around the room, reflecting eerily in the glass jars. The effect was that of a thousand flickering lights bathing the room in light one moment and plunging it into near darkness the next. Ruth would have found it fascinating if she were not so uneasy from the trip through the woods and her earlier conversation with Peter.

They all sat in silence for several minutes. Peter stared around the room, taking everything in as Ruth and Giselle stared at him. Then he stood and prowled around the room, touching this and that.

"I would like to learn what you know," he said at last, picking up a jar of mugwort and examining it.

Giselle glanced at Ruth, a hint of alarm in her eyes. "Why?"

"As a child my parents forbade me to see you. They said you were a witch. They were wrong, and I regret all the time we lost and all the things you might have taught me." He set the jar down and turned back to them. "I've lost everything," he said simply. "But being here, I'm beginning to understand that my greatest loss was the years I missed knowing you."

With tears in her eyes Giselle rose to embrace him. "My darling child, you shall know me, and if it is within my power we shall work together to heal your wounds."

Ruth averted her eyes to give them a moment of privacy. As she did so she prayed that Giselle might really hold the key to Peter's recovery.

They ended up not leaving until the dawn. As they hurried home along the path, Ruth imagined that the trees were shaking their branches at her in anger.

Customers kept Ruth and her father busy for the next several days repairing axes used for wood chopping, making hooks made to hang meat in storage, and taking care of other things that needed to be done before the onslaught of winter. It was a week before she could return to her grandmother's, though she knew Peter had gone several times.

When she entered the forest it seemed peaceful to her. She couldn't remember the last time she had actually felt at home in the woods, welcomed almost. It was a strange sensation, unnerving in itself.

She hadn't gone very far when she heard a voice behind her. "A lady shouldn't walk alone in the woods."

"Who says I'm a lady?" Ruth asked, pulling her dagger from her belt before turning.

"I have," William said, smiling at her.

She returned her dagger to its resting place and relaxed her fighting posture. "Oh, it's you again," she said dryly, unable to stop herself.

"Yes," he answered, striding forward.

She dropped her eyes quickly and hastened to curtsy, her father's warning fresh in her mind.

"A little formal," he commented.

"I'm sorry, milord, you surprised me. I was just hurrying to my grandmother's. If you would excuse me . . ." She turned on her heel and started to walk off, her heart in her throat.

"I won't," he said, his voice growing stern.

She stopped but didn't turn to face him. "*A dangerous*

man," that is what they called him. *"Don't chase strangers in the woods,"* Grandmother said. *What about dangerous strangers? Surely I should avoid them above all!* she thought.

"What's wrong?" he asked, moving to stand in front of her.

"Nothing, milord," she lied, not daring to look at him.

"You know I don't wish to be so formal with you, but if you insist on being so, then I must insist that you tell me the truth. Indeed, I command that you do."

She lifted her head at that, not knowing how to respond.

His eyes bored into her and she grew uncomfortable under his stare.

"Something is different. What is it?"

"I was overly familiar the other day, and I apologize."

"Don't, it was refreshing." He gazed at her more closely, and his eyes narrowed. "Did someone tell you not to speak with me? Your father, perhaps?"

She averted her eyes. "Where is your horse?" she asked.

"I'm afraid I'm alone today."

"The woods are a dangerous place," she warned. He was so close she could feel his breath.

"Not for me," he said in a low growl.

The sound made her shiver. "They told me you are dangerous."

A strange look crossed his face and for a moment he looked in pain. "Whoever told you that was telling the truth."

"And I am a girl alone in the woods. If it is the truth, I would do well to heed their warnings."

He reached out quickly and grasped her forearm. She blanched as she felt his fingers pressing into her muscles. "If you are the same girl I met the other day, then you have little to fear from men in the woods and even less to fear from me."

"And why is that?" she asked, unsure of his meaning.

He smiled slowly. "Because you can take care of yourself. And because I would never consciously hurt you."

And what about unconsciously? she wondered, but she said nothing.

He took a step back and let go of her arm. "Where did you say you were off to?"

"Grandmother's house."

"Then I shall escort you," he said, offering her his arm.

She wanted desperately to trust him, but she also wanted to try and obey her father. "I'm not supposed to talk to strangers," she said finally, in a last effort to avoid prolonged contact.

"Ah, but you and I are hardly strangers, are we? Come, come, I shall be a perfect gentleman."

Despite her best intentions, she laughed and

impulsively took his arm. "You promise not to bite?"

The smile left his face instantly, and she shivered as he stared down at her. "Not today—today you are safe," he whispered.

She felt a chill run through her, and something deep inside her told her that she had seen those green eyes somewhere else. She shook her head to clear it and tried to keep her tone light. "In that case, escort away."

"Your grandmother lives in the woods?" he asked at last.

Ruth nodded. "She was banished before I was born. She was falsely accused of witchcraft."

She felt him stiffen, and fear brushed against her. "Of course that's ridiculous," she hastened to add. "My grandmother studies nature, medicine, the way things grow. Only the ignorant believe in witchcraft."

"I wouldn't be so sure of that," he said softly. "There are more things in this world than can be explained with reason."

"Spoken as a man who has seen some of them," she teased.

"That I have," he whispered so quietly she had to strain to hear him.

They finished the walk in silence, though Ruth was acutely aware of his elbow where it brushed her side and the play of the muscles in his arm beneath her fingertips.

Just before they entered the clearing he suddenly

stopped and turned to her. "I almost forgot, I have something for you."

Ruth tilted her head to the side, puzzled.

From a small bag hanging from his belt he pulled out a rough cross, all four sides equal in length, attached to a chain of thin silver metal. "It belonged to my mother," he explained. "I wanted you to have it as a payment, a thank you, for your help the other day."

"I did nothing more than what was needed," she said, aghast. "And you already paid me for that more than generously."

"No, this isn't for the horse. It is for your kindness. You did much more than you'll ever know. Here," he said, placing it at her throat. "Lift your hair," he commanded.

She obeyed, and he fastened the clasp behind her neck. He moved his hands and she let her hair fall back down. Reverently he touched the cross where it hung low on her throat.

"Perfect," he said. "I want you to have this. I pray to God that it will offer you protection in the days ahead."

She stared down at it for a moment before looking back up at him. "They tell me that none who know you speak well of you. You yourself have admitted to being dangerous. But I don't see that."

He bent down suddenly and kissed her. Almost against her will she closed her eyes and surrendered to his embrace. His lips were warm upon hers and it felt like her whole body was on fire.

She opened her eyes as he pulled away. His own eyes pierced her as he whispered fiercely, "I *am* dangerous."

She blinked, and in a moment he was gone. She turned all around but could see no trace of him, as though he had vanished into thin air. *Just like the man I found on the path.* Her hand flew up to her lips as the realization hit her. *William and the man I found sleeping in the woods are one and the same!*

He cursed himself as he slipped into the forest, hiding from her probing eyes. For the last month he had done nothing but think of her. For a week he had carried the cross with him, debating whether to try and see her, whether to give it to her. He had never thought beyond that. He had never anticipated kissing her.

She had looked so beautiful, so innocent and helpless, and like a wolf drawn to a lamb he had pounced. He could still feel her lips on his, and he knew the memory would haunt him until he died. *She tasted so sweet.*

He was starting to lose control; he could feel it. He had spent years training his mind, learning how to control his thoughts and his feelings. Since the moment they had met he had been reverting, losing his ability to concentrate.

"I am a man, not an animal," he whispered to the forest.

The ancient trees shook in the breeze, denying his

claim. They spoke to him, telling him that he was not what he wanted to be, that he was everything he feared to be. He covered his ears with his hands but could hear them all the same.

"No, I've fought so hard to control myself. I can't let go of that. I must not let passion hold sway." The words sounded empty and hollow even to him.

He turned and fled through the woods back toward the castle. He ran from her and from himself. All he knew was that if he stayed in the woods, he could not be held responsible for his actions.

That night William woke up shaking and covered in sweat. He had had the dream again. He had been in a battle, fighting and killing the dark-skinned men who surrounded him. Their blood sprayed across his chest. His sword was slick with crimson liquid and he fought to keep his hand around the hilt. The fighting ceased for a moment and he stopped to catch his breath. A sound behind him caused him to turn, and he plunged his sword into another man's chest. It was only as he pulled it out that he realized the man was no warrior, just a simple farmer whose land was being desecrated. Next to him his wife stood, screaming in a language he could not understand. She pointed her finger at him, invective flowing out of her small, quivering lips. He knew that she was putting a curse on him, though he didn't know how he knew. A light flashed around him for a brief moment and he blinked. He stared at those sputtering lips, now flecked with foam.

Her lips were still moving after he cut off her head.

Every time he had the dream it was the same. Only upon waking would he remember that it had not been he, but a distant ancestor who had committed the crime. "And unto your sons, for seven generations," he muttered, quoting from the Bible. The sins of his forefather that were being visited upon his head, though, had no such time limit. Every male in his family was cursed, until the end of time. The dead witch had seen to that.

"God forgive me," he prayed, as he always did upon waking from the dream. He dropped his head into his hand and sobbed. The dream was bad enough, but what was coming next was worse. The dream always preceded his three nights of hell. The full moon and the night on either side of it always bore witness to the price he paid for ancient sins.

The sun was streaming into his bedchamber, and he wished, as always, that it would last forever, beat back the cruel moon and rule the sky for eternity. Then he would be free and all his children after him.

He rose and dressed, taking his time, as though that would somehow slow the progress of the rest of the day. He had preparations to make, though, before night fell.

It was growing dark as Ruth reached the edge of the woods, setting out to take a basket of food for her grandmother. She glanced skyward anxiously, seeing that the moon was already up even though the sun had not yet set. *Full moon, or nearly.*

She had hoped to be on her way home by now, but she had needed to stay at the shop longer than she had thought in order to complete an ax. She should hurry if she wanted to get there while there was still some light. *I'll probably have to stay overnight.* She was about to pass the first tree when her foot stopped, hovering in midair.

Something is wrong. She stood, staring, eyes and ears straining. She couldn't see or hear anything amiss, and yet there was. She looked up at the trees, but they stood like silent sentinels. Whatever secrets they had, they kept.

Move forward! she screamed at herself. No matter how much she wanted to, she couldn't will herself to step onto the path. Slowly she lowered her foot back to the ground, next to the other one.

The hair on the back of her neck rose on end. Then, with a swiftness that left her breathless, a wave of fear stronger than any she had ever known washed over her. *Death is in the woods tonight.* She turned on her heel and walked quickly away. *I'm sorry, Grandmother; I will see you tomorrow.*

Her father looked up, surprised, when she entered the cottage. "I didn't expect to see you until the morning."

She thought for a moment about telling him

what she had felt, but she was afraid he wouldn't believe her. Still, she wanted him to know. "It would have been dark before I got there, and, somehow, I had a strong feeling that I should just turn around and come home."

Her father stared at her for a long moment, and she wished that for once in her life she could read his expression. He turned back to the fire he was tending. "Then it is good that you came home," he said quietly.

She stood staring at his back, wondering what exactly he meant by that. She decided against asking and instead put down her basket and changed for bed. "Where's Peter?" she asked after she had laid down.

"He left for your grandmother's several hours ago."

"I'm worried about him," she said before she could stop herself. She held her breath, unsure how her father would respond.

For a long minute he didn't say anything. Finally he sighed. "He's been through a lot. Any man who has seen what he has needs time to rest, recover. He'll be fine."

She heard him stand up, suddenly enough to knock over the stool on which he had been sitting. He swore quietly as he picked it back up.

Biting her lip, Ruth rolled onto her side and stared at the wall, a feeling of unease still lingering with her like the smell of burnt food. She heard her father preparing for bed. Shortly he blew out the lantern and she heard the creaking of the wood as he lay down across the room. Her eyes grew heavy and she closed them. She could feel herself drifting off to sleep when very quietly she heard him say, "I'm worried too."

She opened her eyes but didn't say anything. She couldn't remember a time when her father had ever admitted something like that. She found it disturbing and yet at the same time very comforting. *At least I'm not making that up or reacting to nothing.*

She closed her eyes again and drifted back toward sleep. Then, from way off, she heard the howl of a wolf. She sat upright, heart pounding in fear, and she screamed.

The moon rode full and high in the darkened sky. He could feel it calling to him, illuminating the night, throwing light upon his deeds.

The tanner deserved to die for what he had done to Ruth. That was why he killed him. Alone in the forest there was no one to hear him scream. *He was a fool to be out here alone. He's a dead fool now.* He clawed at the body, slashing clothes and flesh. He picked up an arm and gnawed great chunks out of it. *Must blame it on the wolf. If it weren't for the wolf, it wouldn't have happened. I'm not responsible for the wolf, no man is.*

Ripping, slashing, tearing, rending. *See how the*

claws draw blood, see how the fangs rend flesh. Smell the blood and decay. Already the corpse begins to rot, and all the tiny woodland creatures come to watch. They're all afraid of me.

As they should be.

❖ Chapter Five ❖

Sunlight streamed through the tops of the trees, bathing the path in a golden haze. Ruth skipped along, her basket clutched in one hand and her other wrapped loosely around the hilt of her knife. She was thinking about her cousin and what she could do to help him, and for once she was able to ignore the whispering of the trees.

It was midmorning. Her father was working in the shop all day and had told her to go to her grandmother's early. It was nice to be out of the smoke and the heat. The air was crisp and cold, and she took several deep breaths. Birds were twittering in the trees and darting back and forth across the path before her. They eventually drew her attention away from her dark thoughts.

"It is a beautiful day," she called out lightly to the looming giants surrounding her.

They whispered a reply, but she paid no heed. She paused only to spin slowly in a circle, spreading her arms wide and reveling in the sun upon her face.

When her eyes fell upon a dark form lying just off the path, though, all thoughts of warmth fled. Her heart began to pound and she found herself suddenly drenched in a cold sweat. She dropped the basket, and it landed with a sharp crack upon a branch. She jumped as the sound continued on around her, echoing and only seeming to build in intensity.

She pulled her knife from her belt and advanced with trembling steps. A wind sprung up and the trees rattled their leaves above her. Their swaying caused patterns of light and shadow to play across the ground in a macabre dance.

The dark form was a man, or what was left of him. His throat had been ripped out, and there were deep lacerations and scratch marks all over his body. One arm had been gnawed down to the bone. The ground around him was torn up, with tracks of both a wolf and a man noticeable. The man's blood had seeped into the earth, and drops had scattered upon a few leaves.

His face alone was intact, and by that she knew him. It was Simon, the man with whom she had fought in the shop. His eyes were fixed in horror, his mouth frozen in his death cry.

She fought the urge to fall to her knees and retch. The trees began to shake even more fiercely in the wind, though, and this time their haunting warning was clear to her.

She turned and stumbled back down the path, moving as fast as she could. She snatched up her basket and kept going. A branch snapped behind her, but she was too terrified to look back.

Ahead of her the trees' remaining leaves fell like rain and quickly began to coat the path. She ran through them, wincing as they crackled beneath her feet. Her foot caught on a root that she was certain had not been there the week before, and she crashed to her knees. With a thud, her knife fell from her hand to the ground. Ruth knelt for a moment, panting.

Then she heard it. Something was coming down the path behind her at a steady trot. She turned around and saw a wolf, fangs bared, six feet from her.

She screamed and it lunged at her. She reached for her dagger, knowing that her hand wouldn't find it in time. The beast was upon her, jaws snapping. She rolled to the side and its teeth found only her sleeve. With a tearing sound it came free, and she felt a stinging in her arm where his teeth scratched her.

Then it stopped. It tilted its head and stared at her for a long moment. She stared back, and by his eyes she knew him. It was the wolf that had attacked her as a child. With a cry, she wrapped her fingers around the hilt of her knife, and she swiped at him.

The wolf danced easily out of her reach, though. After a last look at her, it turned and loped off into the trees, her sleeve still in its mouth.

Shaking with fear she pulled herself to her feet, wincing as she put weight on the ankle that had tripped on the root. She stared for a long while into the trees whence the wolf had gone. *Why did he leave me alive?* she wondered. She finally turned and limped the rest of the way.

When she arrived at her grandmother's cottage she was exhausted in both mind and body. When Giselle opened the door and saw Ruth, her face drained of all color.

"Child, what happened to you?"

"It was the wolf from so long ago," she whispered.

Without another word Giselle ushered her inside and bade her sit.

Ruth accepted the chair gratefully and submitted herself to a thorough examination. Within minutes her grandmother had elevated her ankle and put a poultice of willow wood on it, which eased the swelling. Giselle had then washed the scratch on her arm and dressed it with dragonwort to help stop the bleeding.

"The wolf killed Simon the tanner," Ruth said at last.

Giselle looked up sharply. "Are you sure?"

Ruth nodded. "His throat was torn out, his body covered with scratches and partly eaten. There were wolf prints in the dirt, and it wasn't far from there that the wolf attacked me."

Giselle picked up Ruth's left hand and gently pried her fingers open. Ruth stared down numbly as Giselle took the knife from her grasp. She hadn't realized she had still been holding it.

"Did you kill him?"

"No, I didn't even touch him. He tore my sleeve and then he just . . . left."

Giselle's eyebrows shot up in a look of surprise that Ruth had seldom seen from her. "That does not stand to reason."

"Nor did I think so," Ruth admitted.

Outside the wind began to howl angrily around the cabin, shaking the small building in its wrath. "It's an ill wind," Ruth said with a shudder.

"Nonsense," her grandmother snorted. "Wind is neither good nor ill, it just is. Its effects we may not like, but the wind itself bears no will of its own."

"That's not what Father says," Ruth muttered.

"Well, your father's ignorance is not my doing. He's too much like his father—too stubborn to learn, unwilling to believe the evidence of his own senses." Giselle sighed in frustration. "At least you shall know better, whether you choose to follow my path or not."

Ruth smiled at her grandmother. "I will always follow your teachings, in one way or another."

Giselle gazed fondly at her. "That's my good girl. You can also think for yourself, and that is best of all."

Ruth nodded, her fear subsiding with each passing moment. It was good to sit, warm and secure, and bandy words with the woman who had taught her so much.

She leaned her head back and closed her eyes. "I just wish I knew what stayed the wolf's wrath."

"Might have been God, honey."

Ruth opened her eyes and stared in amusement at her grandmother. "I'm not sure I will ever understand your ability to reconcile your unwavering faith with your reliance on only what you can see with your own eyes."

It was an old conversation, but Giselle smiled at her with tolerance anyway. "As I've told you before, the study of nature and the world does not preclude God. You do not see the wind, but you feel it and may know its effects. So it is with God. I do not see the reaction between your skin and the herbs I place upon it, yet I know that it will stop the bleeding faster. I know that it works, even if I do not know how or why."

They fell silent, and once again Ruth listened to the howling of the wind. If she closed her eyes she could almost imagine that it was a hungry wolf prowling around the house and seeking to devour them. She began to shake.

"Tell me of this young nobleman you're interested in," Giselle asked suddenly.

"How did you know?" Ruth asked with a laugh.

Giselle just smiled enigmatically. "I have my ways."

Ruth shook her head. "And I shall never cease to be amazed by them. His name is William, and he is—"

"The earl?" Giselle asked, eyes widening.

Ruth nodded.

"Well, that is impressive. Is he handsome?"

Ruth felt herself blushing. "I believe so. He's tall with brown hair and green eyes. He has wide shoulders, but he carries himself with a grace I've never seen in a man."

Giselle cocked her head. "I believe I have seen such a man in these woods before." She shook her head. "But I cannot be certain of it." There was a moment of silence, and then Giselle asked, "Where did you meet?"

"At the shop. His horse had thrown a shoe just down the street."

Giselle's face took on a look of horror. "At the shop! Well, at least he's seen you at work and there shall be no surprises there."

"Grandmother," Ruth admonished. "I would not have a man who could not at least understand me."

"And it looks like you might finally have found one, heaven be praised."

Ruth began to grow irritated. "Grandmother, I wish you would have more faith in me."

"I do, dear; it's the men I worry about."

Ruth shook her head. "Besides, we barely know each other, and we come from very different backgrounds."

"It wouldn't be the first time a noble married a commoner, if that is what you are worried about."

"It's not just that," Ruth said, shifting in her chair. "It's a great many things. Perhaps if we get to know each other better I will have the leisure to speculate on such improbabilities."

Giselle leaned forward and touched the cross necklace around Ruth's neck. "It looks like it's not a matter of *if*, but rather *when* you get to know each other better." She smiled fondly at Ruth. "You asked me how I knew you had met a nobleman. Only a nobleman could afford to give you such a trinket, and only one with a great interest in you would care to."

Ruth dropped her eyes to the necklace. "You are right," she whispered, admitting it as much to herself as to her grandmother. "I guess I'm just frightened."

"Of what, dear?"

"Losing myself. When I look into his eyes I feel as though I am drowning, and I become terrified. What if he does have feelings for me? What if he even wants to marry me? All I've ever known is fire and steel, and I don't know how I'd give that up. I don't know who I'd be without them."

Giselle clasped her tightly about the neck. "Darling child, what you do does not dictate who you are. Clothed in furs and jewels you would be the same person as you are when covered with ash and soot."

"Do you really think that's true?"

"I know it is. I loved your grandfather, and we were very different people. In loving him, though, and marrying him, I didn't lose myself. Rather, I gained something I had long been in want of. Love makes you more than what you are, not less. Besides, if you're worried that you'll miss 'fire and steel,' you needn't. The fire and steel are in you—they always have been. You need look no further than right here," she said, tapping Ruth's chest.

Giselle stood suddenly, and Ruth thought she caught the glisten of tears in her eyes. "Now let's check those wounds."

Ruth winced as Giselle gripped her ankle, but she had to admit that the pain was less than before, and she could move it freely. "You're a miracle worker, Grandmother."

Giselle smiled. "I like to think so."

Next she checked Ruth's arm. "Bleeding's stopped," she commented. "A couple of days and you won't even see the scratch."

"The same can't be said of Simon," Ruth noted grimly.

A shadow passed over Giselle's face. "No, though I can't say there are many who will miss him."

"Myself included," Ruth admitted hesitantly. It was amazing how quickly her grandmother could distract her from emotional pain as well as physical. As soon as she returned to the village she would have to send men out to recover the body. She shivered. "He was the man I fought with at the shop a few weeks ago."

"Strange that you were the one to find him dead."

"Strange indeed," Ruth whispered, a shiver slithering up her spine.

❦❦ ❦❦ ❦❦

By nightfall the village was in turmoil. The body of Simon the tanner had been retrieved, and everyone had heard the tale of the wolf attacking Ruth. A quick search of the woods near where the body had been found had yielded no wolf, and the searchers had to retreat as darkness crept over the land.

Ruth sat on her bed, feet curled beneath her, and listened to the excited murmur of voices in the street. The door opened and Peter entered, shutting it behind him. He came to stand in front of Ruth. "Are you all right?"

"Yes."

He balled up his right hand into a fist and struck his left palm with it. "I will find the wolf that attacked you and I will kill it," he vowed.

"Thank you," she finally said, unsure how else to answer him.

"They are saying that it is a monster, twice the size of a normal wolf."

Ruth shook her head. "Those weren't my words. He was large, but I wouldn't say he was monstrous."

Peter shook his head, eyes glinting. "Anything that would attack you can be nothing short of monstrous."

She stared at him in the light of the flickering candles, and his face looked strange to her. There was something dark and wild about it. *What has he suffered these many years?* she wondered. More and more he seemed a stranger to her. His joy at being home had been short-lived, and of late she had heard him cry out in the night, only to find him fast asleep. Even his eyes had grown darker, and with each passing day the shadows around them grew.

"Dear Peter, what is it that haunts you so?" she asked, reaching out impulsively to cup his cheek in her hand.

He closed his eyes and leaned slightly into her hand. She held her breath, for a moment believing he might finally reveal his pain to her. He opened his eyes, though, and pulled her hand down. He brushed it lightly with the back of his lips before releasing it.

"Fair cousin, the pain my eyes have seen is not for your ears to hear."

"If not mine, then whose?" she protested.

He smiled darkly. "I do not know, but one day I shall find them and they shall hear their full."

He turned and left the cottage. Alone in the light of the flickering candles she shivered, wondering how long her cousin was meant to dwell in darkness and pitying him for it.

She lay down at last, convinced she would not sleep. As soon as her eyes closed, though, her body slumped and darkness claimed her.

As the sun rose in the sky, William woke. He blinked sleepily for several minutes as he tried to gather his senses. He stretched slowly and stared at his hands, splaying the fingers as wide as he could. Next he stretched his legs, wiggling his toes. At last, with a mighty shake, he sat up and gazed around him.

He was in the woods, but nothing looked familiar. *Where am I?* he wondered, feeling slightly dazed. *I need to find my clothes.*

He tried to think back to the events of the night before, but there was nothing, only a gaping hole where his memories should have been. He felt panic rising in him as he realized that the last two and a half days were completely gone.

Rolling over onto his knees, he saw something that made his blood run cold. With a trembling hand he reached out and picked up the torn remnant of a woman's sleeve.

"Dear heaven, what have I done?" he wailed. He pressed the sleeve to his face and wept. He collapsed back onto the ground, sobbing until there was nothing left in him.

At last the storm passed, and he lay limp and exhausted. By sheer will he finally managed to stand. *I need to find my clothes and go home.*

After a couple of minutes he got his bearings and trudged off through the woods. His bare feet padded on the ground, the soles calloused from many mornings such as this one. After nearly half an hour he reached his destination. He always left his clothes in the same place so that he could easily find them.

Usually he awoke somewhere near them, though that hadn't happened this time.

Why can't I remember anything? What did I do? Questions crowded his mind, and he couldn't cease their clamoring. The moaning of the trees echoed his state.

He spotted his small pile of clothes at the same time he heard whistling. He ducked behind a thick tree just in time to avoid being seen by an older woman. *Ruth's grandmother,* he realized as he watched her. *It couldn't be anyone else.*

The old woman was walking along slowly, a basket on one arm and her eyes fixed on the ground. She suddenly bent over and pulled a plant from the base of a tree. Laying it gently in her basket she straightened and moved on. She was moving ever closer to his clothes, and if she looked up she would discover them.

He bent, picked up a stone, and threw it into the woods in the direction away from his clothes. It landed with a loud thud that startled all the birds into silence.

The old woman didn't turn around; she didn't even flinch. After a moment, though, she said, "If you want your clothes, you're just going to have to come get them."

He could feel the blood racing in him, and he was afraid. How did this woman know that he was here, watching her? He thought about his options. Clearly she couldn't be fooled or diverted. He could leave and come back later. *But what if she takes my clothes with her? Maybe I can make it back to the castle without being seen.* He rolled his eyes. *That's smart—even if I can make it all the way to the castle, there will be eyebrows raised when I walk into the great hall naked.*

He sighed; there was no help for it. "If milady would avert her eyes it would be greatly appreciated."

She raised her head, and he could swear he saw a smile dancing on her lips. "Why? If you feel as free as one of God's forest creatures, then why should you be ashamed to be seen?"

"It was not my intention to be without my clothes."

"Don't fib, young man. There is no water nearby that you might have been swimming in, and your clothes are laid out too neatly for them to have gotten that way by accident."

"Still, I do not wish to be seen."

"You should have thought of that before you decided to take your little romp in the woods."

He shook his head. "You're just as difficult as your granddaughter."

The old woman's smile faded suddenly. "You know my granddaughter?"

"If her name is Ruth, then I know her."

"It is," she said, her voice now cautious. "You wouldn't happen to be the young man she saw naked on the path a month past, would you?"

"I'm afraid so, though I hope she doesn't realize that."

The old woman took on a threatening stance. "You will leave her alone, young man."

William couldn't believe this was happening. He, the earl of Lauton, was naked in the forest being lectured by a peasant woman to leave a lady blacksmith alone. *How much stranger does it get than this?* he wondered. He looked down at the torn sleeve in his hand and wished he hadn't. *A lot stranger, if only Ruth knew.*

"I'm afraid I can't leave her alone. I'm growing quite fond of her." He deepened his tone, something he did rarely. "Now, good woman, you will turn around so that I may get my clothes."

The old woman cocked her head. "Earl of Lauton?" she asked hesitantly.

"Yes."

She turned in an instant. "Beg your pardon, milord."

"All is forgiven so long as you keep your back turned," he said, striding out from behind the tree. He reached his clothes and dressed quickly while she stood silent with her back to him. When he was finished, he debated slipping away quietly but realized there was no longer much use in it.

"All right," he said.

She turned slowly, her face ashen.

"I would prefer it if you did not tell Ruth of this," he said, still in his deepest voice.

She nodded slightly. "It is our secret. Tell me, why?"

"Why do you find an earl in the woods in a natural state?" he asked.

"Yes."

"You wouldn't believe me if I told you."

"I'm not so certain of that. There are things that happen out here that no man can explain."

"Nor woman?"

"Nor woman," she affirmed, shaking her head.

"Let's just say I'm following a family tradition and leave it at that."

She smiled suddenly, and he cocked his head. He had an uneasy feeling that she knew something he would not wish her to know.

"Ruth is right about you," she said softly. "You are different from what one would expect. You did not have to answer my question."

"Ruth is different as well. I've never met anyone like her."

"She's strong, my Ruth. Whatever you have to share with her, she can handle it."

A sense of foreboding filled him. "What makes you say that?"

"I've lived in these woods a long time, seen many things. When Ruth described to me the man who gave her the necklace, I told her I thought I had seen you in the woods before." She paused for a long minute and gave him a sly look. "I wasn't wrong."

He felt his blood run cold. "What do you mean by that?"

"I think the fewer words spoken on the subject, the better," she answered. "Now, if you'll excuse me, milord, I have work to attend to."

She curtsied and turned to go, eyes back on the ground.

William stared at her retreating back as he pondered her words. *How much does she know?* he wondered. *And if I don't tell Ruth, will she?*

He closed his eyes and prayed for calm. The moon was no longer full, but he could still feel its pull on him, and in many ways he was just as dangerous now as he had been the night before. He turned, at last, and began the long journey out of the forest.

Ruth sat on her bed, impatient and fretful. Her father had insisted that she stay off her bruised ankle for another day. It had been three days already, and with nothing to do but relive the attack over and over, she felt that she would go mad. The sun had begun its slow descent in the sky, and she urged it on.

There was a soft knock on the door, and she hobbled over to answer it. A cloaked and hooded figure dashed past her and entered the room. "Close the door quickly, child," a familiar voice whispered.

Ruth hurried to do as she was told. "Grandmother?" she asked wonderingly as Giselle pushed her hood back. Fear rushed through her. Giselle had only braved coming to the village once before, right after the first wolf attack, and it had been she who had done much of the work to heal Ruth's legs.

"Shh, yes," Giselle said, her features tense but her eyes shining with excitement.

"What are you doing here?" Ruth asked. "What's wrong?"

"Nothing's wrong. I came to bring you something."

"What?"

Giselle pulled something from a basket she was carrying. She unfolded it, and in her hands she held a cloak of scarlet.

Ruth stiffened, feeling suddenly faint as she remembered another red cloak she had worn years ago, the day she was attacked by the wolf. She remembered too seeing the dark bloodstains on the tattered garment before her father had disposed of it.

Giselle must have seen Ruth's hands beginning to shake, for she hastened to say, "This one will offer you unique protection from all manner of attackers."

"How?" Ruth whispered.

With a smile Giselle showed her the inside of the garment. There, stitched in the lining, were strips of her brother's armor. Prominently displayed was the crescent moon, still covered with blood.

"It is heavy, but it might one day save your life. As your brother protected you in life so he will in death."

"Thank you," Ruth said, tears springing to her eyes. She stood and tried on the cloak. It was indeed heavy, and the metal banged against her hip, but she felt safe. She closed her eyes and imagined her brother once again beside her, comforting and protecting her. Slowly her image of him faded, though, and was replaced by another. A mischievous smile taunted her, and she found herself smiling as she opened her eyes.

"And how is Lord William?" Giselle asked shrewdly.

"I haven't seen him since you and I last spoke," Ruth admitted. *It's amazing how she can always tell what I'm thinking.*

"It's a gift," Giselle said, smiling.

Ruth shook her head. "Grandmother, sometimes I think you truly are a mind reader."

"If I were I wouldn't admit it."

Ruth spun slowly, favoring her injured foot, getting used to the weight of the cloak and the way it moved. It had an attached hood, and she pulled it up slowly until it covered most of her head.

"It looks beautiful on you," Giselle said.

"Thank you, Grandmother."

"I must go quickly, but you must promise me to always wear it when walking through the woods."

"I will, Grandmother," Ruth assured her, fear once again squeezing at her heart. "Is everything well?"

The older woman's face turned thoughtful. "Let us hope that it is, Ruth. Only time will tell for sure. Now I must go."

"Thank you."

"You are welcome," Giselle answered. She put her hood back up over her head, crossed to the door, and left as quickly as she had come.

After a moment Ruth took off the cloak and sat back down on her bed, clutching the garment in her hands.

❧ Chapter Six ❧

The day dawned dark and ominous. The air hung thick and damp, and no matter how close Ruth stood to the fire she could not drive the chill from her bones. Thoughts of the red cloak haunted her as she made her way to the shop.

Why would Grandmother make me another red cloak, knowing that the first helped attract the wolf? She picked up her hammer and began to pound, imagining that it was the wolf and not metal that she was striking. She had been at work an hour when a shadow darkened the door.

"I was wondering when you were going to show up again," Ruth said as William walked into the shop.

He smiled sheepishly, though his heart began to pound at the sight of her. She stood, sweaty and disheveled, with her hammer poised above a glowing sword. There was no pretense with her, no airs. She was completely natural and completely unaware of how beautiful she looked.

"You never know about me," he joked lamely, not sure how else to answer her. He had desperately wanted to see her, to reassure himself that she was real. So much of his life was dream and illusion, and she seemed the one solid thing he could hold on to. Yet the way she made him feel was anything but ordinary.

In his heart he had also feared that her grandmother had told her everything she knew of him. From the way Ruth had greeted him, though, and the way she was looking at him, it would seem that his secret was still safe.

"You know, my father told me that if I ever saw you in here again I was to run straightaway and fetch him," Ruth said, interrupting his thoughts.

Thinking she was teasing, he answered with a grin, "Well, I guess you'd better do that."

She shrugged. "No need, he's working here today."

A moment later he heard a step behind him. "Is there anything I can do for you, stranger?" a voice boomed close behind him.

William dipped his head to her, almost imperceptibly. *Well played.*

He turned, assuming his best air of authority. "Good day, good sir."

"Father, may I present Lord William. Lord William, this is my father, the owner of this shop."

"A pleasure to meet you," William said.

"We are happy to help you, milord, in any way we can," the blacksmith replied with a skeptical look and a respectful bow.

"I came by to once again thank your charming daughter for the wonderful job she did replacing my horse's shoe."

"I'm glad your lordship approves."

William took in the other man's red face and anxious eyes and realized that the blacksmith was afraid William would disapprove of Ruth's occupation. *How to set his mind at ease and get some time alone with her?* he wondered. The solution came to him and he smiled.

"I would like to engage her services once again. You see, with winter all but upon us, I would like to have all of my horses' hooves checked. I want to make sure they're in excellent condition before the snows. I'm afraid this will be the last chance I have to check on several of them until the spring."

"Of course, your lordship," the blacksmith sputtered. "I always assumed you had your own blacksmith for such things."

"I do, but he is busy with so many other things at the moment that horseshoes seem to be rather low on his list of priorities. Since Ruth did such a splendid job with Shadow, I thought she could take care of all of them."

"How many horses?" Ruth asked.

He turned and smiled at her. "Around a hundred last time I counted."

Her eyes grew large and round, and he had to bite his tongue to keep from laughing at her expression.

"Well, in that case," her father boomed, "she had better get started."

An hour later Ruth was riding beside William in a cart, all her tools in the back and Shadow walking along behind. "That was terribly clever of you," she noted once they were out of earshot of anyone in the village.

"I thought so," he confessed.

"So, are there really a hundred horses in need of new shoes?"

"Yes, actually. I just hadn't thought of having you take care of them until your father surprised me."

She laughed, and he drank in the sound until he felt nearly giddy.

"He's never been happy with my working in the shop, but until recently he hasn't really had any choice."

"What's changed?"

She seemed to sober, and he regretted asking. "My cousin, Peter, returned from the crusade. He was trained as a blacksmith."

"Then he can take your place in the shop."

"He could, but his heart isn't in it; he hasn't been the same."

"Jerusalem broke his spirit?"

"Something did," she said softly.

"I am sorry."

"Me too." After a moment she glanced at him and asked, "Did you ever go to the war?"

For a moment he was back in his nightmare, blood

dripping down his blade. He shook his head fiercely to clear it. "In a manner of speaking," he said softly.

She looked at him with curiosity dancing in her eyes, but she didn't push and for that he was grateful. He twitched the reins, and the pony pulling the cart slowed almost imperceptibly. He wanted to savor the time they had alone before they reached the castle and she went to work.

"How have you been?" he asked, glancing sideways at her.

She reached up and touched something around her neck. He looked closer and with a thrill saw that it was the necklace he had given her. "I assume you heard, else you would not have shown up so quickly," she answered.

Her reply both puzzled and alarmed him. "I have been away the past couple of days. I'm afraid I've heard nothing."

"The night before last a wolf killed Simon, the man I was fighting with that first day we met. I found his body in the woods and then a wolf attacked me."

William cried out and pulled the pony to a halt. "Are you hurt?"

"I'm all right," she reassured him. "The wolf tore my sleeve and scratched my arm. Then he ran off."

I did that, and I couldn't even remember it! he thought, dismayed. *The sleeve I found was hers. Thank God I didn't harm her.*

William balled his hands into fists in an effort

to control their shaking. "I could never live with myself if something happened to you," he whispered.

Ruth sat staring at him, wondering why he was shaking so violently. "What's wrong?"

"Everything," he whispered. He turned, his green eyes boring into her soul. "The last time we met you said that only the ignorant believe in witches. I disagreed with you."

"I remember," she answered, heart beginning to pound.

"I know that there are witches, because my family was cursed by one."

It was her turn to start shaking. Something cold and hard like iron settled in the pit of her stomach, and she began to sweat.

"During the first crusade one of my ancestors killed a peasant farmer and his wife. Before she died, the woman put a curse on every male member of my family."

He stopped speaking and looked at her as though gauging her reaction. She didn't know how he wanted her to respond, or how she should respond, so she sat, quiet and waiting.

"I've never told anyone this," he whispered.

She reached out and touched his hand encouragingly, not knowing what else to do.

"I don't know how to say this," he said, voice filled with anguish.

"You don't have to tell me anything you don't want to."

"Yes, yes I do."

He shook his head, and she watched the struggle helplessly, her heart breaking for him.

Suddenly he reached a hand inside his vest and pulled out a wadded-up piece of fabric. He handed it to her without a word. Puzzled, she took it. When she unfolded it she recognized it as her sleeve.

"This is the sleeve the wolf took from me. How did you get it?"

"I was the wolf."

"What?"

"I am the wolf who attacked you."

Terror filled her in an instant. *He is mad, completely insane!* She wanted to leap from the cart and run back home to her father. *He was right about William all along; he's dangerous and he could hurt me.* Another, more horrible thought occurred to her. *What if he is telling the truth?*

Out loud she stammered, "How . . . how is that possible?"

"The curse placed on all the men in my family is that we turn into wolves for the three nights surrounding the full moon as well as the two days between."

She continued to stare at the bit of sleeve in her fist. With her other hand she rubbed her arm where she could still feel the scratch from the wolf's tooth.

"You?" she whispered.

"Yes," he said, tears streaming down his face. "Can you ever forgive me?"

And then it hit her, why his eyes looked so familiar. They were the eyes of the wolf that had attacked her the day before, the eyes of the wolf that had attacked her nine years before.

Fear and anger coursed through her, and her voice was shaking as she spoke. "Forgive you? For how much?"

In a flash she reached forward and ripped apart his shirt before he could stop her. There, upon his breast, was a jagged white scar. Her heart began to pound even harder, and she thought for a moment she might faint. "How did you get that?" she hissed.

He shook his head. "I don't know. When I was young, I woke up after I had been a wolf, and I had been stabbed with something, I don't know what."

"I know what," she cried, snatching the dagger from her belt. "It was this—my brother's knife. He stabbed you to save my life."

"Your life?" he asked, sounding dazed.

"Yes, when you tried to kill me," she explained, yanking the legs of her trousers up above her knees to show him the scars crisscrossing her legs and the bits of flesh that had been torn out, never to fully heal.

He whimpered and reached to trace a long, jagged scar that ran the length of her calf.

"I didn't know," he sobbed. "I am so sorry."

"For nine years I've carried these scars and fear

has plagued my every step, and all because of you," she spat.

He buried his head in his hands, and the cries that came from him sounded like those of an animal. Ruth sat there staring at him, hatred, anger, love, and pity running through her all at once. Everything but fear.

For once the fear was gone.

She didn't know how long they sat that way. She couldn't even begin to sort out her own emotions, let alone care about his. For a month her world had been in chaos, and now, once again, everything had changed, but in a way for which she never could have prepared herself. The one thing she kept coming back to, though, was the absence of her fear.

"Every day since then I've lived with fear," she said finally. "Never knowing where the wolf was or when he might strike has haunted me. Now, strange as it is, I know where the wolf is and when he could strike. I feel free for the first time in nine years."

He laughed, a strange, strangled sound. "When I was young, I would wake up and never remember anything about what had happened—what I'd done. As I grew older I learned to remember, and then, by the time I was twelve, I could control my actions while in wolf form. What scares me is that this morning I woke up with no memories, and apparently I did horrible things."

"Maybe you didn't kill the tanner," she said, voice

shaking, wishing she believed it herself.

"If not I, then who?" he asked, his voice suddenly fierce. She jerked back, frightened.

"I—I don't know," she stammered. "Maybe another wolf—"

"There are no *other* wolves," he snarled. "The last natural wolves left several years ago. A different pack controls these lands," he added bitterly, "though I'm more a lone wolf with my father so often gone to the Holy Land."

She didn't know what to do. She desperately wanted to comfort him and yet, to her shame, there was a part of her that cried out for his blood. It was this part of her that kept the dagger, its blade naked, in her hand.

She tried to swallow, but her mouth was dry. Her heart had begun to pound again as a war raged within her. She stared down at the knife and her white-knuckled fingers gripping it. *I could plunge this dagger into his heart before he could stop me. I could kill the wolf that took so much from me.* Tears began to stream from her eyes. *I could kill him before he tries again to kill me.*

She didn't realize how hard she was shaking until he reached out and placed his hand on hers, wrapping his fingers around so that he, too, was holding the knife.

"I wouldn't blame you if you did," he whispered, his lips brushing her ear. "I think part of me would thank you."

She sat stunned, staring at their fingers intertwined

around the blade. *Has God or fate brought us to this?* she wondered. *Is this what was meant to happen? Our lives have been entwined for years, though we did not know it. He has been the shadow haunting my steps all along. As the noonday sun kills the shadow, am I the light to destroy his darkness?*

She gripped the dagger even tighter, her nails digging into her palm until she could feel the blood begin to flow. *Twice now I have been in the wolf's jaws and I have escaped. A third time will surely kill me. Should I risk it all? And for what? This tortured man has not offered me anything in return, only a kiss stolen in the forest. Grandmother was right—a girl should not follow a man into the woods.* Her tears fell onto their clasped hands. *But I did not follow him; he followed me.*

She turned to look at him and found that he was crying as well. He kissed her then, their tears mingling on their lips. He wrapped his arms around her, pulling her close and trapping the dagger between their bodies. She could feel the edge cutting her, but she didn't care.

She kissed him with everything she had, every drop of love and anger and pain, and he kissed her back in kind.

"I need you," he whispered against her lips. "You are the light to my shadow, the sun to my moon, the innocence to my guilt. Without you I am lost. If you will not stay with me, then use that knife, because I am dead already."

"I have died a little every day since we met, but

now we shall both live and learn what it is to love," she answered.

She could feel the blade cutting yet deeper into her as he crushed her tighter, but it didn't matter. All that mattered was that he loved her and wanted her, and that his lips upon hers were proving it more with each moment that passed between them.

"All my life I have looked for you," he said.

"And all my life I have run, certain that I would lose myself if ever you caught me."

"Are you lost?"

"I am found." She answered with what was in her heart, her soul.

"What if I devour you?" he asked at last.

She pulled back slightly and touched one of his eyeteeth with her fingertip. "I hope that you do," she breathed.

He glanced down. "You're bleeding."

She looked down as well, noticing with a sense of detachment the slice in her bodice and the blood staining her clothes. She pulled her hand away and let the knife clatter to the floor of the cart. She reached forward to touch his shirt, which was also ripped. "You are as well."

"So I am," he answered, eyes intent on her. "Our blood flows together, Ruth. Even so, you and I are linked, our spirits running together, our hearts beating as one."

"Wherever you go, I shall go."

He gripped her hands, which were covered in their blood, in his and kissed them.

"What do we do now?" she asked next.

"I don't know. I do know, though, that I need your help taming the wolf."

"I'll do what I can," she vowed.

He kissed her again, his lips upon hers burning with hunger, demanding to be fed. In a moment she knew she would be lost, and she would give him everything. She forced herself to break away, though it hurt her more than anything she had ever done.

"William, I can't—"

"I know," he gasped. "I am sorry."

"Don't be, for I am not, but we must venture no further along this particular path."

"Not till I've made you my wife."

She sat, stunned by the sound of the word on his lips. *Wife. He wishes to marry me.* She gazed at him with her heart shining in her eyes.

"What will people say?" she whispered at last.

"They'll say that I'm the luckiest creature that ever walked this earth, on two feet or four."

She laughed, tasting the salt on her lips as she did so. "Whatever shall I do with you?" she burst out, unable to contain her joy and bewilderment.

"You shall marry me, as soon as it can be arranged."

She nodded slowly. "You shall, of course, have to ask my father."

He threw back his head and laughed. "Do you think that he shall deny me as a suitor to his daughter?"

"Perhaps he should," she said with a coy smile.

"Well, then I must strike fast before anyone can warn him. Perhaps while you are tending to the horses?"

She cuffed him lightly on the arm. "You would have your future wife shoeing your horses?"

"You and no other. When we are old and gray I still want to see you, in those ridiculous trousers, putting shoes on all our horses."

"And what is wrong with my trousers?" she demanded.

"They are cut all wrong for your figure," he said with a wicked smile.

She slammed her fist into his chest in mock fury. He caught her hand and pulled it up around his neck. His smile slowly faded. "I am sorry, my love; the humor keeps me from doing to you that which I most wish and which would break your trust."

"I know," she said, the blood burning within her veins. "I feel the same way."

He picked up the reins and turned slowly in his seat. "In that case we had best be on our way, quickly."

They rode the rest of the way in silence. Ruth's mind raced almost as fast as her heart. It was madness to think that this could end happily, with her the wife of an earl. Her thoughts foretold some grave danger ahead of them, even as her heart sang within her breast.

When the castle loomed ahead of them, she held her breath, a thousand emotions colliding inside her. Her mouth gaped in wonder at the castle's sheer size. Within its shadow, stone walls loomed high above her, and she tilted her head back to gaze up at them. Around her, servants scurried to take charge of the wagon and the horses.

William jumped down, and for a moment Ruth stared at him, surrounded by his subjects and the trappings of his title. She quaked inside. *Who am I to aspire to this?*

"Do you really have a hundred horses for me to look at?" she asked, nervously turning her focus to work.

"Probably more," he answered, offering her his hand.

She took it, allowing him to help her down from the wagon. She felt suddenly self-conscious dressed in her trousers as the eyes of all turned upon her.

With a twinkle in his eye William raised his hand, and everyone stopped and stared openly. "This is milady Ruth. She is a blacksmith and will be here looking over the horses. Everyone please extend her whatever help she requires."

Everyone bowed or curtsied as Ruth felt her cheeks grow hot. "William," she murmured for his ears alone. "Was that necessary?"

"Entirely," he whispered back.

She forced herself to smile at everyone, though inside she wanted to turn and run back to the village and her father's shop. *I don't belong here.*

A man her father's age bustled up to them. He bowed low to Ruth, and she, again at a loss as to whether to bow or curtsy, only nodded in return. "I am Samuel," he announced, "and I have charge of the horses."

"Samuel will help you with your work," William said. "He is a good man and has the best eye for horses I've ever seen. There isn't an animal here he doesn't know well."

"Good, then you can tell me which ones kick," Ruth said, glad to be talking business.

Samuel chuckled. "I'll do more than that; I'll hold them for you."

She smiled. "That would be much appreciated, Samuel."

"I'll leave you two to your work. Make sure she finds her way to the hall for supper, Samuel," William instructed.

Samuel bowed again and Ruth just nodded her head again, feeling like an idiot. William turned and strode off, and she heaved a sigh of relief.

Amazing how a mutual declaration of love can cause so much excitement followed by so much awkwardness, she thought.

She pulled a case from the back of the wagon and turned to Samuel. "Lead the way," she said, falling into step beside him. "Lord William said something about a hundred horses."

Samuel snorted. "One hundred thirty-two," he answered.

"This is going to take a couple of days."

He nodded. "A lady blacksmith, eh?"

"Yes. Someone had to help out when my brother left for the crusade."

Samuel nodded. "Figured as much, though it's a shame such a beautiful woman has to work in the dark and heat."

"I manage," she answered shortly.

"I meant it as a compliment, so that you don't mistake me," he said, glancing at her sideways. "I don't doubt your ability to do it."

"Thank you," she said, pleasantly surprised. It was nice to have someone believe she could do the job without her having to prove it.

"We'll start in the barn. We can get twenty done in there. After that we'll have to catch them."

"A long few days," she muttered to herself.

Despite her misgivings, the first twenty were done quickly. Samuel had enlisted the aid of several young boys to hold horses and to begin rounding up the ones that were out at pasture.

They had made a good start before it was time for supper. She would have continued to work, but, true to his word, Samuel saw to it that she made her way to the great hall.

She walked in, sweaty and disheveled, and needed

no more reason to feel completely out of place. When she realized that there were nobles other than William present, she thought about running.

Or fainting. Fainting would work, she thought as William came toward her.

"Glad you could join us," he said.

"William, I'm hardly dressed for this," she hissed.

He looked her up and down slowly, and she flushed at the possessiveness of his gaze.

"Mind your eyes. I do not belong to you," she said, irritated.

"Not yet," he said with a wink.

She stood, anger ripping through her, and did not know how to answer him. She balled her hands into fists at her side and wished she could hit him.

He laughed softly, baring his teeth.

"I hope you are enjoying my discomfort."

"Actually, not as much as you think."

He turned and nodded at a matronly woman who scurried forward. "Please help milady change for supper, as quickly as is prudent."

The woman curtsied and beckoned Ruth to follow her. With a last look at William, Ruth turned and went with her.

The woman led her up a winding staircase into the family's living quarters. They proceeded down a long narrow hallway until they entered a room that was the largest Ruth had ever seen.

A small army of servant women waited inside

with a tub of drawn water, soap, and combs. A dress was laid out upon the bed.

Ruth protested as they laid hands upon her, but her words counted not. They stripped off her clothes with her fighting them the whole way. "I have dressed myself since I was three!" she protested.

They said not a word, but picked her up and threw her in the tub. The water turned dark with dirt and soot. With a sigh she submitted to their ministration. She was soaped and ducked beneath the water twice. Then they hauled her out unceremoniously and began to dry her hair and body. Before she could bat an eyelash they had the dress on her, the bodice binding her tighter than any she had ever worn.

She felt as though her lungs were collapsing. "This won't do," she gasped.

"It will have to do," one of the women told her smartly as two others attacked her hair with combs.

Then, scarcely more than a quarter of an hour after entering the room, she was ready to leave. She hesitantly made her way downstairs, feeling awkward in the clothes, which were not only more restrictive, but also much finer than any she had ever owned. *Is this to be my life?* she wondered in despair, praying not to trip on the hem of her gown.

William stared unabashedly as she entered the hall. She winced slightly as she smiled at him. "Well, what do you think?" she asked as she stood before him.

He smiled. "Beautiful. But, truth be told, I think I prefer you in the other."

"That makes two of us," she said, relieved.

William offered her his arm and she took it. He escorted her to the table and gave her a seat of honor on his right side.

For Ruth the dinner was half dream, half nightmare. There was exotic food the likes of which she had never seen. Barons spoke to her, mistaking her for a noblewoman. Then there was the discomfort of her gown and her own growing sense of unease at being in the place. *I don't belong here and I want to go home.* She forced herself to eat, but the food, delicious as it was, held little interest for her. Her mind was full. Just a few hours before, William had told her a great secret and they had shared something beautiful and frightening. Now that man was gone, and in his place was Lord William, Earl of Lauton, who was bandying words with men who would never deign to speak to her if they knew she was not noble born.

If William noticed her misery, he gave no sign. When the meal was done, the others left one by one until she and William were alone.

"Did you survive?" he asked, suddenly enough to startle her.

"I'm not sure," she admitted.

He nodded, as though he were not surprised.

He rose from the table and she did the same. "I want to show you something," he said at last.

"What?"

He placed his hand gently on her shoulder and turned her around. There, lining one wall of the hall, were the portraits of William's ancestors.

Ruth moved closer to them, William beside her.

She went down the line from the first to the last. When she was done, she walked back slowly toward the beginning and stopped at last in front of one portrait in particular. She tilted her head as she studied it and felt a chill dance up her spine.

"It was he who brought this curse down upon us," William said. "Somehow I thought you would be able to tell."

"I can," she whispered.

"It shows, doesn't it?"

"It's the eyes."

The eyes, indeed. I knew she would see what I see, he thought. He stood for a moment just watching her. *She is so enchanting, so lovely.* He stared at her lips, so full and inviting. The memory of kissing them was nearly overpowering. He took a step forward before he stopped himself. It wouldn't be wise to kiss her in public until their engagement could be announced.

To that end, he needed to speak to her father. *For once I'm grateful for the title,* he thought. *Else what would I say to the man—that I want to offer his daughter a dangerous life with a cursed man?*

He shook his head. "We should get you home," he said, heart heavy with regret.

"I need my clothes back," she answered.

"I'm sorry, but we burned them," he said. He

laughed out loud at the expression of horror that crossed her face. "No," he said at last, "I haven't had them burned. They should be clean by now."

"I'll be right back," she promised as she turned and headed for the stairs.

"I'll be waiting," he answered.

He closed his eyes and pressed his fingers to his temples. *What have I done? What manner of life have I offered her? Death and pain are all the future holds for me, and it is selfish of me to make her share that.*

He opened his eyes and stared in anger at his namesake. Many a time he had wanted to rip the portrait from the wall and throw it into the fire, but never so much as he did now.

Within minutes Ruth returned, looking far more comfortable, and he forced himself to smile. Together, they hurried outside to find the wagon waiting.

"Shall I take milady home, milord?" Samuel asked.

"No, I will escort her," William said, forcing himself to answer.

The ride was long and torturous. He didn't know what to say to her, and she seemed to be experiencing the same problem. He started to speak a half-dozen times only to have the words die on his lips. The horse trotted along, his hoof-falls and the creaking of the wagon the only sounds.

At last they reached the village. "You can drop me off at the shop," Ruth said finally.

"No, I'll take you home," he insisted.

They rolled through the village and she pointed out her home. *How different it is from mine!* he thought.

William climbed down from the wagon. By the time he had reached the other side, Ruth was already on the ground. He slowly lowered the hand that he had extended to help her.

"Thank you," she said.

"For what?" he answered, feeling frustrated.

"I don't know."

He shook his head grimly. "At least that's honest."

She studied the ground for a minute. "There is more work to be done. I will be ready an hour after sunrise."

"I will pick you up then," he said. "Good night."

"And to you," she replied.

Ruth turned without another word and entered her house. William stood for a moment wondering what was wrong with him. He should have taken her in his arms and professed his love, giving her a kiss to dream by. He hadn't, though. All he had managed to conjure up was a weak farewell, no more than he would have given a stranger.

He climbed back into the wagon and turned it around. "I am a fool," he told the horse. "I want her and yet I shouldn't have her. I have her and I don't do anything. I should have at least kissed her. More the fool am I for that."

The horse whinnied quietly and picked up his pace. William leaned back, feeling wearier than he had in a long time.

Halfway home his foot kicked something. He bent down to retrieve it and saw that it was Ruth's knife, still covered in blood. *Our blood*. He picked it up and reverently tucked it into his belt. He would return it to her in the morning.

"How did everything go?" her father asked quietly as Ruth entered the house.

"Well," she answered, giving him a strained smile. She glanced over to the bed used by Peter. He was asleep, snoring gently, and she wondered how late it was.

"How many horses?"

"One hundred thirty-two."

He whistled low. "I can close the shop tomorrow if you need my help."

Ruth was about to tell him that wasn't necessary, but she stopped herself, remembering the nightmarish dinner experience and the silent drive back home. She didn't know if she trusted herself to be alone with William, not just yet. Either she was carried away with passion or she was frozen with fear.

She nodded slowly. "I would appreciate that."

"Done," he said.

Ruth changed for bed and then lay down with a bone-weary sigh.

"Everything else all right?" he grunted.

She didn't have an answer to that. "Everything else is fine."

Slowly she rolled onto her side and tried to push thoughts of William from her mind. It wasn't easy, though. Every time she closed her eyes she saw his face, lit with the fires of love as he looked at her. She could feel his lips on hers and the warmth from his body as he leaned close.

What am I going to do? Am I bound to the words I spoke in a moment of passion? She wasn't even sure she loved him. *Attracted to him, yes. Afraid of him, yes. In love with him? I don't know. And what if I am—what does that mean? Can the two of us have a future that brings anything but pain?*

She rolled onto her back again and glanced toward her father. He was still sitting up, staring into the fire. He looked lost in thought. For a moment she wanted to call out to him, to ask him what she should do.

It was easier when I was a child. There was only right and wrong, and there was no problem Father couldn't fix with a nod or a wave of his hand. That was before the wolf attacked, before Stephen left.

She flipped onto her side. *Maybe Grandmother can help me. Maybe she'll have some advice that I can use.* Ruth shuddered. *She'll tell me that men are trouble, and I finally understand what she means. I need to ask her, though, what made Grandfather different. How did she know she was in love, and how did she know it was right?*

She flopped onto her stomach, the air rushing out of her with a *whoof*. *Maybe the morning will make everything clear, shed a little light into these dark places in my mind.*

❖ Chapter Seven ❖

The morning came, and with it no answers, no magical enlightenment, only more questions than Ruth cared to face. She dressed slowly, reluctantly. She could feel her father's eyes upon her, as though he sensed something was wrong. He didn't ask, though, and she didn't offer to explain.

At last she heard a wagon pull up outside. "He's here," she said, a little more breathlessly than she had intended.

"Sounds like it," her father answered.

"Where's Peter gone to?" she asked, more out of the need to say something than actual curiosity.

"Your grandmother's, I suspect."

Ruth nodded. Peter had spent more time there of late than she had. She hoped that the two of them were getting a chance to know each other, since he had missed out on that in his childhood.

She took a deep breath and, with her father, left the house. Outside William waited, his face pale and drawn. *It looks like he didn't sleep much either.*

She had a sudden mental image of William lying in his bed, and she pushed it from her mind.

"Father agreed to come with me today to help out," she said.

He looked at her in surprise but quickly recovered his composure. "You are most welcome, sir."

"The honor is mine," her father said, bowing.

They climbed aboard the wagon, Ruth sitting between the two of them. The seat was narrow, so they all had to sit close. Her father's knee was touching hers on one side, and William's knee was touching hers on the other.

Well, this is more awkward than I could have imagined, she thought as the silence stretched around them.

At last they reached the castle, and Ruth was all too happy to touch solid ground and move a little way apart from the other two. Samuel was waiting for them and hailed her arrival with a shout and a smile.

"Hello, Samuel," she called warmly.

"And how are you this fine morning?"

"Never better," she answered.

"Who have you brought with you?"

"This is my father, Jacob. Father, this is Samuel. He's in charge of all the horses."

"It's a pleasure to meet you," her father said, his face breaking into a grin as he shook hands with Samuel.

"Likewise. You've raised quite a fine young woman here."

"Thank you," Jacob answered. "Though I can't take all the credit; she's got a strong will of her own."

"So I noticed."

"If you two are quite finished, I believe we have some horses to see to," Ruth interrupted, blushing.

Her father beamed at her, and she could see the

love and pride in his eyes. It hadn't been easy for him all these years, and it was good to know how he felt. She felt a warm glow inside as she set off between the two men.

William watched Ruth as she walked off with her father and Samuel. She was completely in her element talking with them. He turned with a heavy heart and walked inside.

He hadn't slept for thinking of her, wondering and worrying about what he should do. *Since I've met her I have had no peace. No amount of meditation can calm my mind. No amount of logic can calm my heart. I feel my blood run hot within me, and I feel the call of the wolf though the moon dwindles nightly in the sky.*

I feel as though I am losing all that I have struggled so hard to gain—my control, my reason. In the end is she worth it, or will the cost in lives and blood be too much?

No, he was certain that Ruth was altogether worth it, even worth the blood of a hundred others. The question was, did he have the right to make that choice? The blood would be on his head alone. Did he have the right to condemn others so that he could live and love?

He didn't think so, but when he was near her he knew that he would not be able to make the choice to turn away. *The wise path would move me away from her, away from she who holds sway over my heart and slays my logic with a single glance, reduces me to the level of the beasts with a single kiss.*

Two children ran in front of him, and a third, chasing them, bumped into him. He barked at the frightened youngster and sent him scurrying away in tears. He stood for a moment, ashamed of himself. Still, something inside him whispered, *You are the lord of the castle, and he lives by your leave alone. You can bark if you wish; you can kill if it is your will.*

He winced in anguish, struggling against all that was dark in himself. *This is exactly why it is dangerous to have her around. Without her I have more control, I am less dangerous.*

Without her, though, I am miserable, lost, and alone. He paced the cold castle and bemoaned his fate.

With the help of her father and Samuel, Ruth finished by nightfall. Many of the horses were seldom used, and their shoes were still in good repair. No sooner would she finish checking one horse than another would be brought to her, so the work had proceeded quickly. She had pulled off dozens of shoes, filed down hooves, and put on new shoes. All of that had left no time for thoughts of William, for which she was grateful. The work had been hard but altogether satisfying. Still, at its completion, she breathed a sigh of relief.

She was slightly disappointed but not surprised when Samuel entered the castle and returned with a bag of gold and the announcement that he would be taking them home.

On the way the three of them chatted amicably, though Ruth's mind was elsewhere. When at last she made it home, she tumbled onto her bed, fully clothed. Exhausted from her labors, she fell asleep.

She awoke late, and dressed in a clean skirt and blouse. After a moment's hesitation she donned the red cloak. Her father was off already and she didn't see any sign of Peter. After packing some food supplies into a basket, she set out for her grandmother's house. It was only once she set foot into the woods that she realized she didn't have her dagger. Horrified, she froze. *What happened to it?* Then she remembered letting it fall to the floor of the wagon. She closed her eyes and groaned. She would have to see William to get it back.

She opened her eyes and forced herself to start walking. As she strode farther into the forest she began to relax, remembering that for a few weeks, at least, she had nothing to fear.

The trees whispered above her, but they didn't seem to have anything of importance to say. She listened to them and to the few birds who had decided to stay and face the winter's wrath. There was a bite to the air that had not been there the week before.

It feels like snow. Before long winter will be here in full force, she realized. A squirrel ran across the path, his cheeks bulging with nuts for his collection. Soon the furry creature would seek out the warmth of his den and spend the winter feasting on the fruits of his labors.

She smiled to herself and took the extra time to really look around the forest at the creatures surrounding her. In the past she had always raced through at such a pace that she had rarely noticed the comings and goings of the other creatures.

A branch cracked in the distance, and she turned just in time to see a deer slipping out of sight. She stopped for a moment to marvel before moving on again. By the time she reached her grandmother's house she had seen more wonders in the woods than she had ever allowed herself the leisure to see before.

She was smiling as she walked into her grandmother's house. Giselle looked up and eyed her shrewdly, though.

"What's wrong?" she asked bluntly.

Ruth's eyes fell upon Peter, occupying a chair near the fire. "Nothing is wrong, Grandmother," she said in a weak voice. "I just took my time this morning."

"It isn't that which I'm talking about," the older woman huffed. "But we can discuss it later."

Several hours later Ruth took her leave, without having had a chance to discuss William with her grandmother. She and Giselle had spent the time talking with Peter about some of the plants that Ruth already knew about. Peter was still trying to learn all that Ruth had in the years she had been studying. When she left, Peter accompanied her.

Just as they were about to leave the clearing, Mary and James entered it from the other side. They looked startled at the sight of Peter, but after a moment they nodded their heads shyly.

"Who were they?" Peter asked once they were out of earshot.

"Mary and James—friends of Grandmother's."

"Do they study with her as well?" he asked, his tone somewhat sharp.

"You'd have to ask them that," she said cautiously as she looked at Peter.

He didn't look any better. If anything, he looked worse. His hair had grown even longer and was unkempt. His eyes seemed slightly larger, like he was constantly staring at something. His nostrils flared wide, taking in great draughts of air even though he and Ruth were walking slowly.

"How are your studies going?" she asked hesitantly.

"They are not progressing as quickly as I had hoped," he admitted, his voice hard.

"Give it time. The first thing I learned from Grandmother was patience."

"Patience. That is one thing I need no more of," he said, a hint of anger in his voice.

"I didn't mean anything, Peter," she hastened to assure him.

"I know," he said with a sigh.

They walked a little way before he asked, "What all has Grandmother taught you?"

"She's taught me a lot about most of the healing plants that grow in the woods. I've learned how to make poultices to help with swelling, stop bleeding, and reduce pain and fever. I've also learned how the stars are different in the winter and the summer. I've been helping her map them."

"That's it?" he asked, sounding disappointed.

"I don't have as much time to study as I would like," she admitted. "Still, I've learned multiple treatments for all of those injuries, and how to tell if the plants are mature. I like the medicine part, but I found the stars really fascinating."

She fell silent, remembering the nights she had lain out, safe behind her father's house, looking at the stars. *How many of them were full moons? How many of those nights was William wandering the woods?*

She had to stop thinking about William. She returned to the conversation. "What is it you want to learn?" she asked.

"I would like to learn what causes sickness and how to cure it," he said.

"Well, she can certainly teach you that."

"I hope so," he answered.

When they reached the village, Peter veered off toward the house, but Ruth kept walking. She passed the shop without glancing at it.

"Hello, Ruth," the miller greeted as he passed.

"Hello," she responded without looking. Her thoughts were elsewhere, racing ahead of her to the castle. She wasn't sure what she planned to say to William when she saw him. She did know one thing: She wasn't leaving until she got her knife back.

It was a long walk, and she was worn out by the time she reached the castle. As she walked into the forecourt she felt a sudden twinge of misgiving. It had been folly to come here and approach him on his own ground.

Although, this is all actually his ground, she thought. *He owns it all—the land, the village, even the forest.* Suddenly she felt very, very small.

"Lady Ruth!" Samuel walked up to her, leading a white mare.

"I'm no lady, Samuel," she laughed nervously.

"Not the rumor I hear," he said with a wink.

She flushed. "I'm sure I don't know what you're talking about."

"I imagine you're here to see Lord William."

"Wh-what makes you say that?"

"Well, you came to speak to either him or me, and I figured he was the more likely."

She smiled. "As much as I'd like to say I came to speak to you, you're correct. I am here to see Lord William."

"Then let's go find him."

Samuel led her into the castle and through a maze of rooms on the ground floor until they found William. He sat perched behind a large table with parchments spread out before him. His head was bent and he was clearly engrossed in what he was reading.

"Milord, you have a visitor," Samuel said.

Without looking up, William waved. "Show them in."

"Very well, milord," Samuel said, smiling at Ruth on his way out. He closed the door behind him.

She walked forward hesitantly, eyes fixed on the top of William's head. Her mouth was dry, and everything she had rehearsed on her way fled from her memory.

"Milord," she said in a raspy voice that did not sound like her own.

"Yes?" he asked, dipping a pen in ink and scratching something on a paper before him.

"I want my dagger back."

"Who—" he started to ask, looking up. He stopped. "Ruth!"

"Yes."

He jumped to his feet and came around the table. "You look—wait, what did you say?"

"I want my dagger back," she said, forcing herself to smile.

"Oh," he said, looking disappointed. "I thought you came here to see me."

"I did. I came here to see you and ask for my dagger back."

Something flashed in his eyes; whether it was amusement or anger she couldn't tell. In a moment he pulled himself up to his full height, and suddenly she knew she was looking at Lord William and not her friend William.

He strode forward, pulling the dagger from his belt. "You are looking for this." He handed it to her, hilt first.

She pulled at it, but he didn't let go.

"I haven't been able to stop thinking about you," he said softly.

"Really, I haven't been able to tell," she answered truthfully.

"We are all wrong for each other."

"I agree," she said, heat washing through her.

"Since that day we met in your shop, I haven't been able to think rationally. I haven't been able to order my emotions so that I could control the wolf. You have turned my life so upside down that I no longer have control over what I do in that state."

"You are blaming me for your killing the tanner?" she sputtered.

"Indirectly, yes. If you hadn't so distracted me, I would have been able to control myself."

"So it's my fault that you can't control yourself?"

"It is," he said, eyes flashing.

She pulled on her knife, but he held firm.

"Maybe you should be looking no further than your own black heart if you're looking to cast blame."

"This is exactly the reason why I need to stay as far away from you as possible. I can't think straight around you."

He let go of the dagger, and she angrily stuffed it

under her belt. "All you are is a danger to yourself and to me," she hissed, taking several steps backward.

"And when I am near you, all I feel is passion—no logic, no reason, just overwhelming emotion," he spat.

She glared at him as he stepped closer. "We should never see each other again," he said.

"That is fine with me," she said, stepping back again until her back hit the wall.

She stared deep into his eyes, and suddenly she saw something, a change in them. His voice was little more than a growl. "Unfortunately that doesn't work for me."

Then his hands were on her waist and his lips were on hers. She moaned as she wrapped her arms around his neck and gave in to his embrace. She was pinned between him and the wall with nowhere to go even if she had wanted to. *But I don't want to go anywhere. I want to stay here with him, be a part of him.*

He gently bit her lip, tugging on it slightly with his teeth, and she closed her eyes. "It's no use," he said, pulling away ever so slightly. "I tried to forget you, but I can't, not now, not ever. I need you, I don't care what the consequences. Just knowing you, loving you, makes me crazy. If that is my fate, I'd rather go mad with you by my side."

He kissed her cheek and then trailed kisses down her throat.

"We are only going to destroy each other," she whispered. "I should leave now and never return."

"It's too late for that," he said, gazing at her fiercely.

"Why?"

"You love me, don't you?"

"Yes," she whispered. "God forgive me, I do."

"Then I shall never let you go, for I love you."

"I could run."

"I would catch you," he growled against her lips.

"I could kill you."

"Only your absence could do that."

"You can't make me stay with you."

"I will marry you and then you will have to," he said.

"What if I don't agree to that?" something inside her forced her to ask.

He pulled away from her, and his green eyes bored into hers with an intensity that made her quake. "Then I'll make sure your father forces you to marry me."

"And how will you do that?"

"I don't know. I will not lose you, though."

She felt white-hot flame explode throughout her being. "I have no choice but to marry you?"

"None."

She smiled slowly. "Then kiss me again."

William took her home. Together, they rode his stallion. Ruth sat behind him, her arms wrapped around his waist, and she savored the feeling of the wind in her hair. Despite all her work with horses, it was her first time on one, and given the way things seemed to be going, it would not be her last.

Night had fallen, and she gazed up at the moon. It was so beautiful, pale and pristine. She let its light shine upon her face, and she thanked the moon for bringing them together, for without it, they might have always been strangers.

Outside her home William dismounted, and she fell from the horse's back into his arms, laughing. He set her down on her feet. "Are you ready?" he asked.

"No, but that's never going to change."

He nodded and gave her an encouraging smile. "Together, anything is possible."

Ruth took a deep breath and walked inside. Both her father and Peter looked up from the table where they were finishing supper.

"Ruth, who do you have with you?" Jacob asked, squinting to see behind her.

"It's Lord William," Ruth said, her voice catching only slightly.

She felt him move in behind her, closing the door after him. "Hello again," he said, his tone light and conversational.

Jacob and Peter instantly stood and bowed. "Milord, welcome to our home," Jacob said, quickly overcoming his surprise.

Peter, on the other hand, said nothing, but Ruth noticed that he was glaring at William. "This is my cousin, Peter," she said, hastening to introduce them.

"Good to meet Ruth's cousin," William said politely.

Peter only nodded in return, and Ruth was embarrassed. *Why is he acting so strangely?*

"Good sir," William said, addressing her father. "I have come to you to discuss your daughter."

"Do you have another job for her?" Jacob asked.

William smiled. "I do indeed, and it is a far more important one than the last."

"We will be honored to help in whatever way we can," Jacob hastened to assure him.

"It gladdens me to hear you say so. The truth of the matter is, I have come to bargain for a marriage contract."

Jacob's face registered shock, and he turned to Ruth, seeking an explanation. Suddenly his face broke into a smile. "Ah! Samuel, the horse keeper—he wishes to marry my Ruth?" he asked William.

"No, it is not for Samuel that I am here."

"It is for himself," Peter spoke up suddenly.

"Your cousin is very astute. It *is* for myself that I am seeking this. I wish to marry Ruth."

Jacob's face went completely white. Ruth stepped forward and took his hand. He turned to look at her, mute.

"It is true, Father. William and I are in love, and I wish to marry him."

"Have you gotten her in the family way?" Peter hissed.

William turned on him, nostrils flaring. "If you

knew your cousin at all, you would not dare to ask that."

The two locked eyes, and the hair on the back of Ruth's neck stood on end. She heard a slow growling begin to fill the room, and what scared her most was that she wasn't sure which one of them it was coming from.

"Enough!" Jacob said, and both younger men snapped their eyes back to him. "This is a happy occasion and blessed news. I would be honored to give you my daughter in marriage."

William smiled and stepped forward. "It will be my honor to call you father," he said.

The two embraced, and Ruth's joy was complete. Tears of happiness slid down her cheeks. She turned to glance at Peter, though, and was instantly chilled to the bone. He was glaring at the two men, his eyes wide and practically shining in the darkness. She shivered and wrapped her arms tight about herself, striving to keep out the chill.

News of their engagement having finally been made public, they were to be married in four and a half weeks' time. Ruth felt like singing as she stood hammering out a new sword, her wedding gift to William.

Her grandmother had been delighted for her, although not surprised. She had hinted that there were things about William that Ruth should know. Ruth had replied that she knew all of William that she needed to. Her grandmother seemed suspicious, but Ruth dared not reveal her newfound secret about William's family, at least not yet.

As the news had spread the villagers had begun to treat her differently. At first she had found it unnerving and tried to make them stop, but she had finally grown to accept it. There were even whispers that her grandmother might be able to return to the village. Everyone was eager to embrace the girl who would marry the earl, even if it meant overlooking their fear of her grandmother.

The one dark spot in her happiness was Peter. For the last three weeks he had haunted her steps, watching her like a hawk. Whenever William was close by, Peter would be extra alert and aggressive.

From his stool in the corner of the shop Peter spoke. "I think Grandmother is holding things back from me."

"What do you mean?" Ruth asked cautiously.

"I think she knows more than she is willing to tell."

Ruth sighed, not liking the direction this seemed to be heading. "Maybe she doesn't think you're ready to learn them yet."

"Not ready? Not ready! I spent nine years in hell itself, and she thinks I'm not ready?"

Ruth put down her hammer and resolutely turned to face him. "Peter, what is it that you want?"

"I want to return and avenge Stephen!" he practically shouted. "And myself," he added so softly that she could barely hear him.

She flew to him. "Peter, what are you saying? You can't go back there. I can't lose you, too!"

He gazed at her, and for a moment she saw in his eyes the boy who had gone off to war so long ago. "You already have, Ruth," he whispered. "God help me, I might as well have died on that battlefield too."

❧ *Chapter Eight* ❧

Slash, claw, bite, kill. Angry trees shouting above; ignore them, ignore them. Trees don't touch me, can't hurt me. The woman tasted sweeter than the man, but the man had more meat on him. Destroy, devour, the wolf will have his fill.

Blame the wolf, always the wolf. Never me, just the wolf. Watch him kill, blood will spill. Growling, snarling, clawing, biting.

All are dead.

All are dead.

"Wolf!" the cry went up through the streets. "Wolf! Wolf!"

Ruth heard the shout and ran outside. She caught the arm of a boy running by and asked him, "What's happened? Who is dead?"

"A man and a woman found just now, their throats torn open."

"And what of the wolf?" Ruth cried. "Did anyone see the wolf?"

"No, but they're going to find him."

Ruth released the boy's arms, and he continued running up the street, shouting all the way.

"*Think!*" she said to herself frantically. *Was the full moon last night or the night before?* Her brain was racing so fast that she couldn't remember. She forced herself to take several deep breaths, trying to clear her mind. *The night before—the full moon was the night before. That means there will be no wolf for them to find today.*

She sagged in relief against the wall of the building and clasped the cross between her fingers. "Oh, William," she whispered, "what have you done now?" Just then she caught sight of the grizzly cavalcade bringing the bodies into the middle of town. She didn't want to look, but she was drawn to the wagon against her will. As she stood above the bodies a fresh wave of horror gripped her, for she recognized Mary and James. She backed away with a cry and turned and ran toward the woods.

She fled into the forest, taking the path toward her grandmother's house. A light dusting of snow covered the ground—the first snowfall of winter. It was not enough to hinder her progress, but she chose her steps carefully.

Halfway down the path she turned sharply and plunged into the woods. William had told her that he kept clothes near that spot. She hoped he was still there.

"William!" she cried as she ran. "William, where are you?" She stopped running at last and fell to her knees. "William," she gasped, "are you here?"

"I am," a tired voice said behind her. She rose and fled into his arms.

"What is it?" he asked as she sobbed against his chest.

"Mary and James are dead."

"Who?" William asked.

"Mary and James. They were my grandmother's students. They were found this morning with their throats torn out."

"I'm sorry, I'm so sorry. It's all my fault," he said, looking stricken.

"Do you remember anything?" she asked, gazing up into his face.

"Nothing," he answered.

"Maybe it wasn't you."

"Who else could it have been?

"The next full moon, I'll stay with you. I'll watch you. Maybe I can prove that you are not doing this."

"Dear Ruth, what if I hurt you?" he cried.

"You won't; we'll find a way, I promise. I have to go and tell my grandmother what has happened. Meet me tomorrow."

"Be careful," he begged.

"I will," she promised. She turned and left while she still could. By the time she reached the path, tears were running down her cheeks. Whether her tears were for the dead or the living, she did not know. She'd gotten herself under control by the time she reached her grandmother's house.

Her grandmother opened the door, and upon

seeing Ruth's face cried out, "What's wrong?"

"Mary and James have been killed. They think a wolf did it."

Giselle's face crumbled, and she collapsed into Ruth's arms. Ruth held her as she cried, her own emotions hopelessly chaotic. Perhaps it was time to tell her grandmother the truth. Maybe, just maybe, she could help.

The storm passed at last, and Giselle dried her tears. She looked at Ruth. "Was there something else you wanted to tell me?"

"Yes," Ruth admitted, not even asking her how she knew.

"Does it have something to do with Lord William?"

Ruth nodded.

"The wedding is still on, isn't it, child?"

"Yes."

"Then what is it?"

"Grandmother, you know how you've always taught me to question everything, to find the reasonable explanation for everything?"

Giselle nodded, eyes fixed on her.

"Well, there is no reasonable explanation for what I'm about to tell you. . . ."

Giselle raised an eyebrow but said nothing.

"William's family was cursed during the first holy war in Jerusalem. Every male of the family has wolf blood running in his veins. The light of the full moon takes them over, and they run in the forest, a wolf in the eyes of beasts and men."

Her grandmother blinked and seemed to accept the news in stride. She looked somber for a moment, then asked, "And you fear that it is he who has been killing of late?"

"He fears it, though I do not wish to. I do know that he was the wolf that attacked me when I was a child."

"Then he is the young man who roams the forest without clothes," Giselle mused.

"Yes. He used to be able to control his actions in wolf form, but of late he has not even remembered what he has done."

"His passion for you has clouded his mind," Giselle guessed.

Ruth nodded, trying not to blush.

"Then the two of you have a very serious problem. I do not know if there is anything I can do to help."

"But you do believe me?"

"Of course I believe you." Giselle pulled her granddaughter close. "Sometimes the fantastic is the logical explanation. Your love was cursed by a witch. We will accept that and move on."

"I am sorry," Ruth said, anguish filling her.

"Do not be sorry, just promise me that you will be careful until we can figure out what to do."

"I will, Grandmother."

"Go now. I need some time to think. Come back next week and we shall talk some more. In the meanwhile, be happy, child. The days of happiness in one's life are fleeting and should be treasured. Hold tight to your William, for he will need you now in his hour of darkness."

Ruth kissed her grandmother's cheek and took her leave. She hurried home, a shadow chasing her footsteps and sadness eating at her heart. The trees were silent, offering no words of wisdom or comfort or warning. She wished that they would. When the trees whispered, she never felt alone.

She remembered she had once told her grand-mother that she thought the trees spoke to her, and that occasionally a tree she knew well would be in a different place. *Like the root that seemed to spring up out of the ground to trip me the day the wolf tore my sleeve.*

Her grandmother had told her that trees were liv-ing things given to constant change and that the for-est itself could be different from day to day. She had told her, though, that the trees did not move about and that they whispered only to themselves and not to her. Ruth remembered being both relieved and a little disappointed.

"I wish you could tell me what happened last night," she addressed the trees. "Was it truly my William or something else?"

The trees kept their secrets. *Maybe they're afraid to tell me, knowing that I do not want the truth they could share.*

William wasn't ready to leave the woods, not just yet. It took him a little over an hour to find the place where the man and woman had been killed. Standing there, staring at the blood-soaked ground, he felt sick to the bottom of his soul.

The imprint of two bodies was visible in the snow. Around them were the tracks of an animal; prints of giant paws tipped with deadly claws jumbled together with the footprints of the man and woman.

He sank slowly to his knees and touched his hand to the scarlet snow. "God forgive me, for I know not what I've done."

"William?" He heard Ruth's voice soft behind him.

He turned and saw her standing a few feet away. He reached his hand out to her and she came and took it. Together they kept vigil, into the dark hours of the night. A light snow began to fall, coating them both with wet flakes.

They spoke not a word, she standing and he kneeling, both staring at the marks of violence. He realized her strength was deep, far exceeding his own. Somewhere in the darkness he vowed that another would never die because of him.

"You'll help me?"

"Yes," she answered.

Ruth crept into her house before the dawn could break, trying hard to be silent. She slipped into her nightclothes and lay down, gritting her teeth as the bed groaned slightly beneath her.

She rolled over and nearly screamed when she saw Peter staring at her in the darkness. He was lying still on his bed, silent, but his eyes spoke volumes.

He knows I was with William, Ruth realized. He still does not trust him, and he certainly thinks that we were up to no good. I wish there were something I could say to change his mind.

There wasn't, though, and she knew it. *Maybe it's because it was William's father that he and Stephen followed off to war; maybe he resents the whole family because of what happened to them there.*

Peter turned his head slowly and deliberately away from her, and she felt a cold emptiness inside. Somehow she knew that there in the darkness she had lost him. *He has slipped away from me and I don't think he will ever return,* she realized, heart heavy with grief.

At last she turned away too, unable to help feeling bad as she literally and figuratively turned her back on him. *He is beyond my reach and beyond my help. He doesn't trust me anymore because of William.*

She drifted to sleep, praying that there was still hope for Peter.

The days fled swiftly by, filled with work and wedding preparations. She barely saw William for a week. When she did see him, it was only to discuss wedding business, and they were never alone.

Ironic that now we are engaged we are so heavily chap-

eroned, she thought. She gave up at last and came to grips with the fact that between her family and his servants, they would not be alone again until after the wedding.

Except I must find a way to be alone with him on the nights of the next full moon, which will end just two days before our wedding. He will need me then, and no force can keep me from helping him.

She mopped her brow and stepped outside the shop for a breath of fresh air. She was just in time to see William riding into the village. *Think of the devil and he shall appear,* she thought bemusedly. *Though I pray he is not the devil we both fear he is.*

"Beloved," he called, loud enough for half the village to hear.

She blushed, still not used to being called that, nor used to the gawking stares it always brought from passersby.

"Milord," she answered.

"You know, you need to stop calling me that."

"I'll stop calling you that in public after we are married. In private I shall call you whatever I like," she replied tartly.

"Feisty this morning," he said, chuckling as he slid from his horse. He took a step forward as though he meant to kiss her, when her father came out of the shop, clearing his throat.

Only Ruth saw William roll his eyes, and she quickly bit her lip to keep from laughing out loud.

"Good father," William greeted Jacob.

"Milord," Jacob answered.

"You can call me son," William suggested.

"I'll call you that when you are wed to Ruth and not a moment before. Until then, you are milord."

William sighed in an exaggerated manner. "I see where she gets it from. Pray tell, neither of you harbor any illusions that I might try and back out of the wedding?"

"I don't believe you will, milord. You seem to be an honorable man, if nothing else. It just wouldn't be right."

Ruth watched in fascination as William set his jaw. She knew that her father still did not wholly trust him in all things. He still believed that William was a dangerous man with a hot temper, but he did believe that William was honorable. It was a start, at least. Still, for a while there would be no more familiar embraces between the two men like the one they had shared upon sealing the engagement.

She was enjoying the fresh air, but she knew that if she tried to speak with William outside, her father would stay and less work would be done. Shoulders slumping, she turned and led the two men back inside. At least there she and William could speak and her father could work, content that he was performing his chaperone duties.

"What have you come about?" she asked.

"Your presence is requested by the dressmaker tomorrow afternoon."

"I'm going to be at my grandmother's tomorrow. Can we make it the day after?"

"We can do anything you wish," William said, looking for all the world like he was going to try kissing her again. He shot a glance at her father, whose back was turned toward them, and then he swooped down and gave her a swift peck on the cheek.

He stepped back hastily, but not before her father could say, "I heard that."

Ruth couldn't stop herself from laughing.

"I'm sorry, Father," William said, giving her a wink.

"I also had the cardinal send a message to my father, informing him of our wedding. It will reach him after we are already wed, but he will be glad to hear that I have taken a bride."

A lump formed in Ruth's throat at the thought of the Holy Land and the crusade. "Do you think your father will return home soon?" she asked.

William shook his head. "To be honest, I don't know. He has spent most of his adult life there. I don't know why, exactly."

He gave her a look, though, that told her he was pretty sure why and that it had something to do with the family's secret. She nodded to show that she understood.

"I look forward to meeting him whenever he does return," she said. *If he does return*, she thought to herself, knowing personally how easily he might not.

❖ Chapter Nine ❖

The trees were whispering again as Ruth hurried toward her grandmother's. She couldn't tell what the trees were saying, but it made her scurry even faster, feet flying across the crunching snow. Two weeks had passed since Ruth had told Giselle of William's curse. When she had gone last week to try and discuss it further, she had been frustrated in her purpose by the presence of Peter.

Peter arrived before she did, and he left after she did as well. These days he looked gaunt, his hair pulled back with a leather tie. He had been growing his beard out, and it was at the length that made him look a little wild and unkempt. He paced the room constantly, reminding Ruth of the squirrel that had spent three hours accidentally trapped in the cottage the summer before.

Ruth had wished to discuss him with her grandmother as well, but she didn't have the chance. *Today, hopefully, things will be different.*

When she reached the clearing, she noted how silent everything seemed. A ripple of unease went through her as she knocked on the door. There was no answer.

"Grandmother," Ruth called as she opened the door. She walked inside, and her blood ran cold. Everywhere glass jars lay smashed on the floor. Her grandmother's worktable was turned over, its contents scattered everywhere.

"Grandmother," Ruth whispered, terror filling her.

A groan from the corner drew her attention. There lay Giselle, blood trickling from the corner of her mouth and shards of broken glass covering her clothes. Ruth dropped to her knees and cradled her grandmother's head.

"Who did this to you?" she gasped.

Giselle could only manage a gurgling sound.

"What did they do to you?"

Again there was no answer. Giselle's eyes closed and her body slumped.

"Grandmother!" Ruth screamed.

Giselle did not stir, but Ruth noticed with relief the steady rise and fall of her chest. At least she was still alive. Ruth gently eased her grandmother's head back down on the ground and stood up. *Somewhere in this house there is something that can help me; I just need to figure out what it is.* She crossed to a shelf whose jars were still intact and studied the contents.

Three hours later Ruth had cleaned up the house as best as she could. She had moved her grandmother to the bed and had done her best to make her comfortable. She had applied a poultice to her grandmother's wounds and was trying to decide what to do next.

Outside the wind howled like a ravenous wolf, rattling the shutters as though seeking a way in. It was then that Ruth truly understood that she was wrestling not with nature or injury but with death itself. She raised her fists to the sky. "You cannot have her," she cried to wind and dark and death. Just then there was a knock at the door. She flung open the door, half expecting hell itself to be on the other side. Instead it was William, his face twisted in concern.

"I waited for you for hours," he said. "Is anything wrong?"

"Everything," she said. "Someone attacked Grandmother."

"What!" William exploded, pushing past her into the cabin. "Is she okay?" he asked.

"I don't know. I'm not sure what I can do to help her."

William knelt by her grandmother and laid his ear to her chest. "Her heartbeat is slow, erratic," he said after a moment. He glanced up. "Could she have been poisoned with something here?" he asked.

"I'm sure she was, but I don't know with what," Ruth said, cursing herself for not being able to think clearly.

"We can take her to the village healer."

"No!" Ruth exclaimed. "She is not welcome in the village. Also, she and the healer never saw eye to eye. She would rather die than have him treat her."

"Well, she might just do that," William said

grimly, rising to his feet. "Tell me what I can do."

"Go tell my father what has happened," she begged.

Her father came, but there was nothing he could do other than look helplessly at the still body of his mother. At last he went home, tired and upset. Peter didn't come, but sent word that he would help out her father while she took care of their grandmother.

For Ruth, it was a long, sleepless night filled with worry. The next morning she sat by her grandmother's bed, grateful that Peter had offered to help her father in the shop for a few days. She was surprised that he hadn't offered instead to come and keep watch over Giselle, though. *Maybe he's seen too much death and illness,* she thought.

Ruth continued to work on finding a cure for the one woman who could have told her what to use. "Come on, Grandmother, wake up. I need another lecture," she pleaded softly.

It's not fair that the one person who could fix all this is the one person who can't, she thought.

She had racked her brain time and again thinking of all the poisons her grandmother had warned her about. None of them seemed to match Giselle's symptoms.

She rose and walked about the room, stopping to look again at each jar, each potted plant, and each drying herb. *The answer is here, I know it,* she thought, frustrated.

She sat again and took a deep breath. Mentally

she ticked off once more all the poisons she knew. Then, at last, it came to her. *The day I came to tell her Stephen was dead. What was she talking about?*

Monkshood.

That is it!

"God, please let me remember how to treat it," she prayed.

Grandmother said it was incredibly deadly. A small amount could cause numbing, a tiny bit more death. She also went on to say something about slowing the heart, causing paralysis. . . .

She struck her fist into her open palm. If it could do that, surely it could render someone unconscious.

With renewed purpose she made the rounds of the cottage, searching for the cure. *I don't remember what it was, but hopefully something will jog my memory.*

When she came across the digitalis, she remembered. "I have to fight poison with poison," she said out loud, beginning to feel sick with anxiety. "I could kill her, but if I do nothing, she will die anyway."

She turned, determined, and crossed back to her grandmother. She placed a piece of the poison plant in her grandmother's mouth and washed it down with a small sip of wine. *She said something about alcohol being good for treating both of them. Let's hope she was right.*

Ruth waited anxiously for some sign. Nothing happened for nearly an hour, and then, suddenly, Giselle began to vomit.

Ruth panicked but quickly rolled her grandmother

onto her side and helped clean out her mouth. The older woman's chest began to heave and her skin grew warm to the touch, a marked difference from her clamminess that morning.

Suddenly her eyes flew open, the blue almost totally obscured by the black orbs in the centers. They were enormous, but some part of Ruth told her that this was right.

Giselle reached up and grasped Ruth's hand for a moment. She squeezed it hard before her own hand fell back to her side and her eyes closed. Her body slumped again and Ruth feared the worst. Giselle's chest still rose and fell steadily, though.

Ruth put her ear to her grandmother's chest and cried for joy when she could hear her heart beat, steady and strong. *It is working! Hold on, Grandmother, you're going to be okay after all*, Ruth thought.

She sat back up with an overwhelming sense of relief. As she stared at her grandmother's body, however, she realized that they weren't out of the woods yet.

Over the next several days her grandmother awoke off and on, usually just long enough to take a sip of water. She still couldn't speak, but she smiled up at Ruth, her eyes expressive, before she would slip back into her slumber.

Ruth longed to ask her what had happened, who had attacked her, but her grandmother was never conscious for long enough. *Not that she could answer me anyway.*

The days passed and Ruth's anxiety grew. William visited several times, always accompanied by her father. Ruth managed to joke that her grandmother wasn't much of a chaperone in her state, but it was hard to feel cheerful.

Still, the wedding plans were laid, and her father managed to get work done at his shop. The world moved on without Ruth. But as the full moon drew near again Ruth began to fear. She had never been able to discuss with her grandmother what to do to help William.

At last, the night before William was to transform, Giselle awoke and was able to stay conscious. She tried to speak but could not yet, her throat still raw from her ordeal. The next afternoon Ruth felt she could leave her alone, at least for a few hours, while she tended to the wolf.

❧ Chapter Ten ❧

The trees were anxious. They looked down upon the man and woman in the woods and watched as she chained him up with great and mighty chains. One of the trees volunteered his trunk as an anchor for the chains, but he did not believe they would hold.

The trees had seen the man before, and they knew what he was capable of. They knew that in his other form he had hurt the woman twice. They fretted for her, but there was nothing they could do. Her course was set and she would not be swayed. The trees sighed mournfully.

There is only the wolf now, there is no more me. Killing, fighting, hide who you are, but not forever. She could help him, but she wouldn't; and for that she was going to pay.

"Are the chains tight enough?" Ruth asked, testing them one last time.

"They feel secure now, but I do not know if they will hold once I am transformed."

"It's a chance we're just going to have to take," she admitted, even though she didn't like it.

"It would be safer if you left," William urged. "I don't want you to be hurt."

She shook her head emphatically. "We will never know for sure unless I stay and keep watch."

He leaned forward and kissed her. "You are as wise as you are brave."

"You forgot beautiful," she teased.

"Well, that one was a given," he said, smiling. He looked up at the sky and his smile slowly faded. "The sun is going down."

"So it is," she murmured, looking at the darkening sky. She bent forward and kissed him, and she prayed that it wasn't for the last time.

She then moved a little distance away, out of his reach, and sat down with her back to another tree. The first snow of the year had thawed and the ground was dry once more. She carefully wrapped her scarlet cloak around her, grateful for the protection it offered and only slightly saddened by the memory that it was her brother's armor that lined her cloak and kept her safe. Once seated, she pulled out her dagger and clutched it tightly in her hand.

Next to her on the ground was an extra change of his clothes. For modesty's sake he had foregone his usual practice of undressing before transformation.

"Don't forget, the wolf can sense fear," he said by way of a final caution.

As the last light of the lingering sun left the sky, Ruth felt a shock go through her. She shivered and turned her eyes to William.

He lay, body contorting and convulsing upon the ground. She bit her tongue to keep from screaming. She heard the sound of rending fabric, and soon gray tufts of fur began to peer through his clothes.

"William?" she whispered despite herself.

She heard the cracking of bones as his body reformed itself. Snarling and whimpering sounds that could not be made by a human came from the writhing form. She closed her eyes, unable to bear it any longer.

When the sounds had subsided, she opened her eyes to find that William was completely gone and in his place stood a large wolf. She shivered and involuntarily pressed her back harder against the tree, her body seeking an escape route.

When the animal threw back its head and howled at the moon already rising in the sky, it was the most frightening sound she had ever heard. She gasped as a shiver raced up her spine.

The wolf turned suddenly toward her, its large green eyes on her. *William's eyes. I don't know why I never realized it before.*

The creature lunged at her, and with a scream she raised her knife up in front of her to protect herself. The chains held, though, and brought him up short. He strained at them, snarling and snapping not four feet from her. His massive paws dug into the ground, tearing it up.

She wanted to scream but forced herself to try

and remain calm. "All is well, William. Be still. It is only I, Ruth, and you know I mean you no harm."

The creature continued to claw and snap, and despite her best efforts she began to remember what it was like when those same teeth had ripped chunks from her flesh and those same paws had slashed her legs.

"I am not afraid of you," she whispered, willing it to be true. "You are William, my love. You just need to be still and remember yourself."

The wolf stopped snarling for a moment and cocked its head, as though considering her words. She held her breath, praying that she had reached him. After a moment, though, he lunged at her again.

Then, just as suddenly, he gave up, turned, and ran the other way. The chain brought him up short again, with a yelp that pained her. He threw himself in that direction for only a moment before repeating the action in other directions.

Ruth watched, fascinated. He didn't venture near her again, and for that she was very grateful. At long last the wolf lay down and closed its eyes.

"That's right, my beauty, just go to sleep. Rest and I'll wait here to keep watch."

Ruth woke with a start, light shining in her eyes. She sat up slowly, unable to remember where she was. When she saw the chains looped around one of the massive trees, she remembered.

"William!" she cried.

The wolf was gone.

She jumped to her feet and grabbed the end of the chain in her hand. One link had been gnawed clean through. "He's free," she whispered, horrified. Above her the trees moaned.

She turned and ran as fast as she could to her grandmother's house. The path seemed to stretch out forever, and behind her trees whispered, urging her to hurry. Somewhere close by a wolf howled, and she screamed.

Maybe this is it. Maybe we will finish what we started so long ago. Maybe the wolf will kill me, but it won't be easy. She clutched the dagger even tighter in her fist.

When she reached the cabin she burst inside, panting. "Grandmother, something horrible has happened!"

"It certainly has," an unfamiliar voice snarled.

She turned and saw Peter, hovering over their grandmother's bed. She could barely recognize him, though. He was hunched over like an animal about to pounce, his face was twisted in a hideous snarl, and his eyes were enormous. In his hand he clutched a wolf's paw, and there were scratches on Giselle's face, around the eyes, which must have come from the claws.

"You shouldn't have come."

"Peter, what are you doing?" Ruth asked, overwhelmed.

"The old woman knows what I want but she won't give it to me. She hides secrets, magic, and she won't teach me."

"Peter, I've told you, there is nothing magic about what Grandmother does. It all revolves around study of the plants and animals.

"Quiet!" he bellowed. "That's just what you'd like me to think. Maybe you're hiding the secrets from me too. *They* were, you know. They wouldn't tell me, even when I killed them."

"Mary and James?" Ruth asked.

"Yes. They died with the lies still in their teeth."

"I told you," Giselle wheezed. "There are no secrets, no magic."

"Liar!" he shrieked. "There must be."

"Why do you want magic so badly?" Ruth asked, slowly trying to approach him.

"To take it back to Jerusalem and use it to defeat our enemies and avenge us." Her cousin was drenched in sweat, shaking with rage.

Giselle shook her head weakly. "I could have taught you many things, Peter, but not this."

Peter raised the paw as though to swipe at her again.

Desperate, Ruth called out, "Peter!"

"What?"

"Your eyes are so big. Have you taken any of Grandmother's medicines?"

"No," he snarled. "My eyes help me see in the dark the hidden things people don't want known. Like your potential husband. My eyes help me see right through him, and I know his secrets."

Remain calm; he can probably sense fear, she told herself.

151

She glanced at his face again, trying to judge what he would do next. His lips were open and pulled slightly back from his teeth. *They look so sharp, like an animal's teeth. The only way they could look like that was if someone had filed them.*

She remembered the files they used in the shop and felt a fresh wave of horror burst through her. *He thinks he's an animal!*

"Put down the wolf's paw," Ruth said gently.

"Why? This is the paw of the wolf that we dragged from the forest nine years ago, the one that almost killed you."

"That wasn't the wolf that attacked me," Ruth said before she could stop herself.

Just then a great gray ghost slipped into the cabin through the door that Ruth had left open. "*He* is," she whispered, her mouth dry with fear.

Peter turned to look at the creature, and Ruth took advantage of his momentary distraction to throw herself forward. She knocked the paw from his hand and brought her dagger up. He gripped her wrists and began to wrestle with her. Suddenly he swept his foot behind her ankles and tripped her, sending her crashing to the floor. She landed with a gasp as all the air rushed out of her body. Her knife went sailing into the air.

Peter leaped and managed to grasp it. With a roar he dropped down and brought the dagger to bear on her chest. He tried to plunge the dagger in, but it went only the barest amount and then stopped with a metallic clang.

Stephen's armor! Ruth thought wildly as she grabbed the hilt of her dagger and kicked upward into Peter's chest with all her might. *Grandmother was right that this cloak would save my life.*

The kick was enough to send him flying, and he lost control of the dagger. Ruth picked it up with a roar and was about to fling herself at him when a gray streak brushed past her.

She stood and watched in shock as the two fought each other: her William who had been cursed to take the form of a wolf, and her cousin who had taken on the mind of a wolf. With a roar they came together, locked in combat.

Within moments it was over and the wolf stood above Peter, fangs dripping with blood. Ruth's knees gave way beneath her and she collapsed onto the floor. The wolf turned to look at her and then stalked over toward her. He stared into her eyes for a long minute and then lay down at her feet, his head resting on her boot.

⋇ Chapter Eleven ⋇

Peter was buried quietly, one last victim of the wolf attacks. Ruth herself told the villagers how Peter had bravely fought the wolf, and that each had mortally wounded the other. Her father took the truth hard, but he understood and accepted it. He also accepted William, though it was clear his fears had only multiplied.

Her grandmother was fully recovered. Before Ruth had made it back to the cottage, Giselle had managed to drag herself from her bed and treat her remaining injuries, including taking something to restore her voice.

It had been Peter who had attacked her, sure that she was a witch and trying to kill her when she told him she had no secrets to share with him. He had been using the wolf's paw as a weapon—an extension of himself and a symbol of his slide into madness. In the end Ruth believed he had truly seen himself as an animal.

It has been a traumatic couple of weeks, but at least Father, Grandmother, William, and I are all together now, and we are all safe.

She smoothed her hands down the sides of her dress. *And through it all my wedding gown even got made. Though, truth be told, I'd rather be wearing trousers. At least I convinced them not to tie it so tightly that I can't breathe.*

She still couldn't quite believe everything that was happening. The unknown future stretched out before her like a dark forest. Thanks to William, though, she had gotten over her fear of dark forests. So, although she still felt uncertain, she didn't feel afraid.

I don't know if I'll ever feel like a lady, she thought as she climbed down the stairs toward the great hall. *But I've got a lifetime to try.*

It was two hours before the wedding, and she had managed to escape her attendants, at least for a moment. In the great hall she saw her grandmother deep in conversation with William.

"We may never know who killed the tanner," Giselle said just as Ruth walked up.

Her grandmother turned and beamed at her. "There you are, dear, and you look radiant."

"Thank you."

William reached for her hand. "I was telling your grandmother that I remember everything from the last wolf cycle—the chains, the fight, everything. Now that I can remember, I should be able to slowly start to control myself again."

"Does that mean your passion for me is waning already?" Ruth teased.

"On the contrary," he said, eyes burning with fire. "My love for you has given me the strength to be a better man, even a better wolf. In time maybe I'll have more control over the whole process than ever."

"Oh no, that will not do at all," Giselle said with a sly grin. "That is why I have brought you two the perfect wedding present."

"What is it?" Ruth asked.

Giselle smiled enigmatically and then turned and removed one of the portraits from the wall. Ruth noted with interest that it was the portrait of the man who had brought the curse down upon William's family.

Ruth and William exchanged puzzled looks as Giselle walked across the room. "Grandmother, what are you going to do?"

Without answering, Giselle suddenly threw the portrait upon the fire. Ruth flew forward with a cry, but William stopped her with a hand on her arm. Together, they watched as the picture burned. At last it was gone, and Ruth turned to look at the wall where it had hung.

"Look!" she gasped.

William spun around, and he saw it too. "They all look different, changed somehow."

Giselle smiled as she turned back from the fire. "They are, and so are you, William."

He turned completely white.

"William, what is it?" Ruth demanded, totally bewildered.

"You're right, I can feel it. The curse is gone," he whispered fiercely. "The curse is gone!" he shouted, picking her up and spinning her around.

"How do you know?"

"I know. I can feel it."

A surge of love and joy washed through Ruth. The days stretched ahead of them filled with sunlight, and the shadow was finally gone. She kissed William with all the passion in her heart, and he kissed her back.

"Nothing can ever come between us," he whispered.

She laughed through tears of joy. At last she turned to her grandmother, who stood watching with a twinkle in her eye.

"Grandmother, how did you do it? How did you break the curse?"

"Magic."

❖ Author's Bio ❖

Debbie Viguié is the author of *Midnight Pearls* and the coauthor of the Wicked series. When not busy writing, Debbie spends her time visiting theme parks with her husband, Scott, and relaxing with friends and family. Debbie lives in the San Francisco Bay Area. Her Web site is www.debbieviguie.com.

New adventures are
just around the corner!

Turn the page to read an excerpt from the next book
in our fairy tale program . . .

SUNLIGHT AND SHADOW
by Cameron Dokey

AVAILABLE JULY 2004
from Simon Pulse

❧ ❧

$\mathcal{M}$y mother was silent, gazing up at the light streaming out from my father's room—silent for so long, I became all but certain she wouldn't answer at all. Then, just as I was beginning to feel altogether wretched, she said:

"Yes, we loved each other. Once. It might even be the case that we still do. It's been so long since I've thought of such things that I no longer know. But I do know that your father and I have never understood one another. And without understanding—"

My mother broke off, her eyes still fixed on the light.

"Love is like water, Mina," she continued, after a moment. "Water, in all its forms. It can squeeze between your fingers like your own tears. Burn and freeze your heart at the same time. It can evaporate before your very eyes in no more than an instant. Making a reservoir to hold your love is the most difficult task in all the world. You will never do it if you do not understand first yourself, and then your beloved.

"Have you heard the saying 'Still waters run deep'?"

"Of course I have," I said.

"But do you understand its meaning?" asked my mother. "It's the best way I know to describe abiding love. Remember that phrase when your father marches his parade of potential husbands by you. Look for the place within, the reservoir where love may reside until it fills to overflowing. Do not be dazzled by outside appearance, for that is merely what the sun does best: It shines."

"I will remember," I promised.

"Good," said my mother. Then she turned and laid her hand against my cheek. "Go inside now. Sleep and have sweet dreams, my daughter, for tomorrow is a big day. You will be sixteen and I must take you to meet your father."

"Yes, but will you?" I asked, intending to tease, for my mother had never gone back on her word as far as I knew. Not to me, nor to any other. I knew that she would keep her part of the bargain made at my birth, no matter what it cost her.

She laughed, but the sound was without mirth.

"Now you sound just like your father. His greatest fear all these years has been that I'll change my mind at the very last minute, find some way to keep you all to myself."

"He doesn't know you very well, then," I remarked.

"On the contrary," a new voice said. "I know your mother very well."

With a cry, my mother spun around, thrusting me behind her. Not that it did any good, for in the same instant, torches flared to life all around us as if the very ground had opened up and spewed forth fire. And so, in the space of no more than a few heartbeats, we were surrounded by my father's soldiers.

I think my mother understood what he intended at once, though I wasn't far behind her. There could be but one cause for this: My father intended to take me away before the appointed time.

"No," my mother said—a statement, not a plea. "Not this way, Sarastro."

"It is the only way I can be sure," the voice said, a voice I now recognized as my father's. "And I've had almost sixteen years to think about it."

A figure stepped forward. In one hand it carried the largest, brightest torch of all—so bright, it made my eyes water and caused my mother to muffle her face inside her cloak. My first true sight of my father was thus obscured by tears, and I learned a lesson that I never forgot.

Darkness may cover light, but that is not the same as putting it out. Whereas all light need do is to exist for darkness to be overcome.

Yet even beaten back, my mother was not cowed.

"This is not the way, Sarastro," she said again. "There is no need to do this, and the day may come when you will be sorry you have made this choice."

But my father simply laughed, the sound triumphant and harsh.

"Don't think you can threaten me with words, Pamina," he said. "It is simple. I have won, and you have lost. It was never much of a contest in the first place, really."

"It should never have been a contest at all."

"Enough!" my father cried. "I will not stand around in the dark and argue with you. Instead I will simply take my daughter and go."

At this, I saw him give a signal, and I braced myself. I expected several soldiers to try to drag me from my mother's side. Instead a single man stepped forward. Even through the water in my eyes, I could tell he was the most handsome man that I had ever seen. Eyes the color of lapiz lazuli. Hair that shimmered in the torchlight, almost as bright a gold as mine. He extended one hand toward me, as if inviting me to dance.

"Give me your hand and come with me," he said. "And I swear to you that your mother will not be harmed. Resist, and there is no telling what will happen."

And, in this way, I learned a second lesson I never forgot: Beauty may still hide a treacherous heart.

"What do you take me for?" I asked, and I did not hold back the scorn in my voice. "I will not give you my hand, for to do so is to give a pledge. This I think both you and the Lord Sarastro know full well.

"I will not be tricked into pledging myself to a stranger. But I will come with you for my mother's sake, for I love her well and would not have her harmed."

"Strong words," my father said.

"And a strong mind to back them up," my mother replied. "I say again, you will regret this act, Sarastro. Thrice I have said it, and the third time pays for all."

"Step away from your mother, young Pamina," the Lord Sarastro said. "I will not ask again. Instead I will compel."

And so I stepped away, pulling my hood down over my face, for I had begun to weep in earnest and did not want to give my father and those who did his bidding the satisfaction of seeing me cry. The second I stepped away from my mother, I could feel the wind begin to rise, tugging on my cloak with desperate, grasping fingers, howling like a soul in hell.

Over the scream of the wind, I heard my father shouting orders in a furious voice. Then I was gripped by strong arms, lifted from my feet, and thrown like a sack of potatoes over someone's shoulder.

The last thing I saw was the flame of my father's torch, tossing like some wild thing caught in a trap.

The last I heard, dancing across the surface of the wind like moon on water, was a high, sweet call of bells.

"Once upon a time . . ."

is timely once again as fresh, quirky heroines breathe life into classic and much-loved characters.

Reknowned heroines master newfound destinies, uncovering a unique and original "happily ever after...."

Historical romance and magic unite in modern retellings of well-loved tales.

✦✦✦✦✦

THE STORYTELLER'S DAUGHTER
by Cameron Dokey

BEAUTY SLEEP
by Cameron Dokey

SNOW
by Tracy Lynn

MIDNIGHT PEARLS
by Debbie Viguié

**Season Howe is a witch on the run
for a horrible crime that happened**
three centuries ago—a crime so awful, her punishment will last forever.

Daniel Blessing is the handsome stranger who has spent a lifetime hunting the evil witch.

Kerry Profitt, an innocent college student, doesn't believe in witches at all.

But Daniel's quest is about to bring Kerry and Season together in the strangest of ways—a way that will make Kerry believe all too well. . . .

Summer. Fall.
Winter. Spring.

Four seasons,
one incredible
adventure.